Praise for
Kristine Kathryn Rusch

"Rusch is a great storyteller."

—*RT Book Reviews*

"Whether [Rusch] writes high fantasy, horror, sf, or contemporary fantasy, I've always been fascinated by her ability to tell a story with that enviable gift of invisible prose. She's one of those very few writers whose style takes me right into the story—the words and pages disappear as the characters and their story swallows me whole....Rusch has style."

—Charles de Lint

"A masterful writer is at work."

—Orson Scott Card
New York Times bestselling author

"Rusch's greatest strength...is her ability to close down a story and leave the reader feeling that the author could not possibly have wrung any more satisfaction out of the piece."

—*The Kansas City Star*

"Rusch is a great storyteller—easily the equal of Patterson or Koontz."

—*Analog*

"Kristine Kathryn Rusch is one of the best writers in the field."

—*SFRevu*

"[Rusch's] writing style is simple but elegant, and her characterization excellent."

—Mark Morris
Beyond

"Kristine Kathryn Rusch's crime stories are exceptional, both in plot and in style."

—Ed Gorman
Mystery Scene Magazines

Praise for the Retrieval Artist series

"If you love puzzle mysteries, crime novels, well-invented sci-fi worlds, or stories about characters you can believe in and care about, you owe it to yourself to give Rusch's Retrieval Artist novels a try."

—Orson Scott Card
New York Times bestselling author

"What links [Miles Flint] to his most memorable literary ancestors is his hard-won ability to perceive the complex nature of morality and live with the burden of his own inevitable failure."

—*Locus*

Praise for the Smokey Dalton series
(writing as Kris Nelscott)

"Nelscott's series setting, in the turbulent late '60s, gives her books layers of issues of racism, class, and war, all of which still seem to remain sadly timely today."

—*Oregonian*

"Nelscott has her own, very distinct voice, and her series creates its own deeply satisfying pleasures and cogent points."

—*Seattle Times*

"Nelscott is good at conveying the edgy caution that blacks once brought to their movements among white society."

—*Houston Chronicle*

"(A) crime writer deliberately taking chances."

—*Chicago Tribune*

"It's not hard to draw parallels between Nelscott's PI Smokey Dalton and Walter Mosley's Easy Rawlins, another secretive, canny black man trying to solve mysteries while circumspectly navigating the white world. But Dalton's no knock-off. (Would you label the hundreds of hard-boiled detectives who've appeared in Raymond Chandler's wake mere Marlow Xeroxes because they're white?)"

—*Entertainment Weekly*

Also by
Kristine Kathryn Rusch

Bleed Through
Snipers
Five Mystery Stories (a collection)
Five Diverse Detectives (a collection)

The Retrieval Artist Series:

The Disappeared
Extremes
Consequences
Buried Deep
Paloma
Recovery Man
Duplicate Effort
Anniversary Day
Blowback

The Smokey Dalton Series (as Kris Nelscott):

A Dangerous Road
Smoke-Filled Rooms
Thin Walls
Stone Cribs
War at Home
Days of Rage

Five Female Sleuths

Kristine Kathryn Rusch

Five Female Sleuths

Published 2013 by WMG Publishing
www.wmgpublishing.com

Cover design by Allyson Longueira/WMG Publishing
ISBN-13: 978-0-615-77135-9
ISBN-10: 0-615-77135-1

"Discovery," by Kristine Kathryn Rusch was first published in *Alfred Hitchcock's Mystery Magazine,* November, 2008.

"Cowboy Grace," by Kristine Kathryn Rusch was first published in *The Silver Gryphon*, edited by Gary Turner and Marty Halpern, Golden Gryphon, 2003.

"Jury Duty" by Kristine Kathryn Rusch was first published in *Crimewave 8*, 2005.

"Patriotic Gestures" by Kristine Kathryn Rusch was first published in *Scene of The Crime*, edited by Dana Stabenow, Running Press, 2008.

"Spinning" by Kristine Kathryn Rusch was first published in *Ellery Queen Mystery Magazine*, July, 2000.

WMG PUBLISHING
www.wmgpublishing.com

Contents

Five Female Sleuths

Kristine Kathryn Rusch

Introduction

I HAVE ALWAYS had a vivid imagination, a writer's imagination. From my earliest memories, I inserted myself into whatever narrative I found. Then, when I became a teenager, those narratives grew darker.

After I watched *Wait Until Dark*, in which Audrey Hepburn played a blind woman who had to defend herself against thieves who broke into her apartment, I walked around the house with the lights out and my eyes closed, wondering how I'd fare. While I read one of the Alfred Hitchcock mystery anthologies (I believe it was *Stories to Read with the Lights On*) one night when I was home alone, I heard a strange wailing. Instead of waiting until my parents got home, I acted like the classic horror movie heroine, climbing up the stairs to investigate. I did, however, take off my shoes and avoid the creaky parts.

Turned out to be the wind wailing in a half-open window. But I was *scared* and determined to be heroic at the same time.

Of course, had the wailing been something else, I would have been in deep trouble, just like any horror movie heroine. So it's better for me to write about the things I imagine instead of act upon them.

The five stories in this collection all come from moments in my life, moments when I imagined myself in a different situation.

Shamus nominee "Discovery" came out of a train wreck that a few of us, including my husband Dean Wesley Smith and writer Scott Edelman, witnessed as we left the Jack Williamson Lectureship at Eastern New Mexico University. There were no lawyers or shotguns, but we did see a lot of dead cattle.

Edgar nominee "Cowboy Grace" came from an incident that occurred with my old high school friend Janine Plunkett McCusker. I had moved away from our hometown, and she had stayed. Our friendship, once close, became the stuff of Christmas cards and the occasional letter. I sent her a copy of a book I had dedicated to her, and received a heartbreaking letter from her husband, saying she had died of breast cancer. We had become so far apart that I never even knew she was ill. The bad friends in this story aren't based on Janine; they're based on me.

Some of real life appears in "Jury Duty." The opening conversation in the jury room actually happened on one of my stints on jury duty in my small Oregon county. I have to say, though, that I am not on the run, and I did not move to the Oregon Coast to hide.

"Patriotic Gestures," also an Oregon story, comes from my own ambivalence about protests and protest movements. I'm fascinated with the way opinions change from decade to decade, even inside one person.

Both "Jury Duty" and "Patriotic Gestures" appeared in year's best anthologies.

The final story, "Spinning," is also an Edgar nominee, written while I was taking a class in that particular torture. My instructor was female, though, and she was a little more lenient than the instructor in this story. I didn't lose as much weight as Patricia, either, probably because I wasn't nearly as determined.

I can't say these five stories saved me from my horror heroine impulses. They more closely resemble that moment when I staggered around the house, eyes closed, bumping into furniture to see if I would survive.

The five women featured in these stories all fared better than I would in similar circumstances. They're tougher than I am—and thinner, too.

—Kristine Kathryn Rusch
Lincoln City, Oregon
August 13, 2010

Discovery

"Over there." Pita Cardenas waved a hand at the remaining empty spot on the floor of her office. The Federal Express deliveryman rested a hand on top of the stack of boxes on his handcart.

"I don't think it'll fit."

It probably wouldn't. Her office was about the size of the studio apartment she'd had when she went to law school in Albuquerque. She could have had a cubicle with more square footage if she'd taken the job that La Jolla, Webster, and Garcia offered her when she graduated from law school five years before.

But her mother had been dying, and had refused to leave Rio Gordo. So Pita had come back to the town she thought she'd escaped from, put out her shingle, and had gotten a handful of cases, enough to pay the rent on this sorry excuse for an office. If she'd wanted something bigger, she would have had to buy, and even at Rio Gordo's depressed prices, she couldn't afford payments on the most dilapidated building in town.

She stood up. The Fed Ex guy, who drove here every day from Lubbock, was looking at her with pity. He was trim and tanned, with a deep West Texas accent. If she had been less tired and overwhelmed, she would have flirted with him.

"Let's put this batch in the bathroom," she said and led the way through the rabbit path she'd made between the boxes. The Fed Ex guy followed, dragging the six boxes on his hand truck and probably chafing at the extra time she was costing him.

She opened the door. He put the boxes inside, tipped an imaginary hat to her, and left. She'd have to crawl over them to get to the toilet, but she'd manage.

Six boxes today, twenty yesterday, thirty the day before. Dwyer, Ralbotten, Seacur and Czolb was burying her in paper.

Of course, she had expected it. She was a solo practitioner in a town whose population probably didn't equal the number of people who worked at DRS&C.

People had told her she was crazy to take this case. But she was crazy like an impoverished attorney. Every other firm in New Mexico had told her client, Nan Hughes, to settle. The problem was that Nan didn't want to settle. Settling meant losing everything she owned.

Pita took the case and charged Nan two thousand dollars, with more due and owing when (if) the case went to trial. Pita didn't plan on taking the case to trial. At trial, she wouldn't just get creamed, she'd be pureed, sautéed and recycled.

But she did plan to work for that two grand. She would spend exactly one month filing motions, doing depositions, and listening to offers. She figured once she had actual numbers, she'd be able to convince Nan to take a deal.

If not, she'd resign and wish Nan luck finding a new attorney.

Her actions wouldn't hurt Nan. Nan had a spectacular loser of a case. She was taking on the railroads and two major insurance companies. She had no idea how bad things could get.

Pita would show her. Nan wouldn't exactly be happy with her lot—how could she be, when she'd lost her husband, her business, and her home on the same day?—but she would finally understand how impossible the winning was.

Pita was doing her a favor and making a little money besides.

And what was wrong with that?

***

AT ITS HEART, the case was simple. Ty Hughes tried to beat a train and failed. He survived long enough to leave his wife a voice mail message, which Pita had heard in all its heartbreaking slowness:

"Nan baby, I tried to beat it. I thought I could beat it."

Then his diesel truck engine caught fire and he died, horribly alive, in the middle of the wreck.

The accident occurred on a long stretch of brown nothingness on the New Mexico side of the Texas/New Mexico border. A major highway ran a half mile parallel to the tracks. On the opposite side of the tracks stood the Hughes ranch and all its outbuildings.

Nan Hughes and the people who worked her spread watched the accident. She didn't answer her cell because she'd left it on the kitchen counter in her panic to get down the dirt road where her husband's cattle truck had been demolished by a fast-moving train.

And not just any train.

This train pulled dozens of oil tankers.

It was a miracle the truck engine fire hadn't spread to the tankers and the entire region hadn't exploded into one great fireball.

Pita had been familiar with the case long before Nan Hughes came to her. For weeks, the news carried stories about dead cattle along the highway, the devastated widow, the ruined ranch, and the angry railroad officials who had choice (and often bleeped) words about the idiots who tried to race trains.

It didn't matter that the crossing was unmarked. Even if Ty hadn't left that confession on Nan's voice mail (which she had deleted but which the cell company was so thoughtfully able to retrieve), trains in this part of the country were visible for miles in either direction.

The railroads wanted the ranch, the cattle (what was left of them), the life insurance money, and millions from the ranch's liability insurance. The liability insurance company was willing to settle for a simple million, and the other law firms had told Nan to sell the ranch, and pay the railroads from the proceeds. That way she could live on Ty's life insurance and move away from the site of the disaster.

But Nan kept saying that Ty would haunt her if she gave in. That he had never raced a train in his life. That he knew how far away a train was by its appearance against the horizon—and that he had taught her the same trick.

When Pita gently asked why Ty had confessed to trying to beat the train, Nan had burst into tears.

"Something went wrong," she said. "Maybe he got stuck. Maybe he hadn't looked up. He was in shock. He was dying. He was just trying to talk to me one last time."

Pita could hear any good lawyer tear that argument to shreds, just using Ty's wording. If Ty wanted to talk with her, why hadn't he told her he loved her? Why had he talked about the train?

Pita had gently asked that too. Nan had looked at her from across the desk, her wet cheeks chapped from all the tears she'd shed.

"He knew I saw what happened. He wanted me to know he never would have done that to me on purpose."

In this context, "on purpose" had a lot of different definitions. Ty Hughes probably didn't want his wife to see him die in a train wreck, certainly not in a train wreck he caused. But he had crossed a railroad track with a double-decker cattle truck filled carrying two hundred head. He had no acceleration, and no maneuverability.

He'd taken a gamble, and he'd lost.

At least, Nan hadn't seen the fire in the cab. The truck had flipped over the train, landing on the highway side of the tracks, and had been impossible to see from the ranch side. Whatever Ty Hughes's last few minutes had looked like, Nan had missed them.

She had only her imagination, her anger at the railroads, and her unshakeable faith in her dead husband.

Those were not enough to win a case of this magnitude.

If someone asked Pita what her case really was (and if this imaginary someone could get her to answer honestly), what she'd say was that she was going to try Ty Hughes before his wife, and show her how impossible a defense of the man's actions that morning would be in court.

And Pita believed her own powers of persuasion were enough to convince her jury of one to settle.

***

BUT THE BOXES were daunting. In them were bits and pieces of information, reproduced letters and memos that probably showed some kind of railroad duplicity, however minor. A blot on an engineer's record, for example, or an accident at that same crossing twenty years before.

If Pita had the support of a giant law firm like La Jolla, Webster, and Garcia, she might actually delve into that material. Instead, she let it stack up like unread novels in the home of an obsessive compulsive.

The only thing she did do was take out the witness list, which had come in its own envelope as part of court-ordered discovery. The list had the witnesses' names along with their addresses, phone numbers, and the dates of their depositions. DRS&C was so thorough that each witness had a single line notation at the bottom of the cover sheet describing the reason the witness had been deposed in this case.

The list would help Pita in her quest to recreate the accident itself. She had dozens of questions. Had someone inspected the truck to see if it malfunctioned at the time of the accident? Why had Ty stayed in the truck when it was clear that it was going to catch fire? How badly had he been injured? How good was Ty's eyesight? And how come no one helped him before the truck caught fire?

She was going to cover all her bases. All she needed was one argument strong enough to let Nan keep the house.

She was afraid she might not even find that.

DRS&C's categories were pretty straightforward. They had categories for the ranch, the railroad, and the eyewitnesses.

A number of the witnesses belonged to separate lawsuits, started because of the fender benders on the nearby highway. About a dozen cars had damage—some while they were stopped beside the road, and others because they'd been going too fast to stop when the train accident occurred.

Pita started charting the location of the cars as she figured this category out, and realized all of them had been in the far inside lane, going east. People who had pulled over to help Ty and the railroad employees had instead been dealing with accidents involving their own cars.

A separate group of accident victims had resolved insurance claims: their vehicles had been hit or had hit a cow that had escaped from the cattle truck. One poor man had had his SUV gored by an enraged bull.

Cars heading west had had an easier time of things. None had hit each other and a few had stopped. Of those who had stopped, some were listed as 911 callers. One had grabbed a fire extinguisher and eventually tried to put out the truck cab fire. That person had prevented the fire from spreading to the tankers.

But the category that caught Pita's attention was a simple one. Several people on the list had been marked "Witness," with no accompanying explanation.

One had an extra long zip code, and as she entered it into her own computer data base, she realized that the last three digits weren't part of the zip code at all.

They were a previous notation, one that hadn't been deleted.

Originally, this witness had been in the 911 category. She decided to start with him.

***

C.P. WILLIAMS was a Texas financier of the Houston variety, even though his offices were in Lubbock. He wore cowboy boots, but they were custom made, hand-tooled jobbies that wouldn't last fifteen minutes on a real ranch. He had an oversized silver belt buckle and he wore a bolo tie, but his shiny suit was definitely not off the rack and neither was the silk shirt underneath it. His cufflinks matched his belt buckle and he twisted them as he led Pita into his office.

"I already gave a deposition," he said.

"Before I was on the case," Pita said.

His office was big, with original oil paintings of the Texas Hill Country, and a large but not particularly pretty view of downtown Lubbock.

"Can't you just read it?" He slipped behind a custom-made desk. The chair in front was made of hand-tooled leather that made her think of his impractical boots.

She sat down. The leather pattern bit through the thin pants of her best suit.

"I have a few questions of my own." She took out a small tape recorder. "I may have to call you in for a second deposition, but I hope not."

Mostly because she would have to rent space as well as a court reporter in order to conduct that deposition. Right now, she simply wanted to see if any testimony was worth the extra cost.

"I don't have that much time. I barely have enough time to see you now." He glanced at his watch for emphasis.

She clicked on the recorder. "Then let's do this quickly. Please state your name and occupation for the record."

He did.

When he finished, she said, "On the morning of the accident—"

"I never saw that damn accident," he said. "I told the other lawyers that."

She was surprised. Why had they talked with him then? She was interviewing blind. So she went with the one fact she knew.

"You called 911. Why?"

"Because of the train," he said.

"What about the train?"

"Damn thing was going twice as fast as it should have been."

For the first time since she'd taken this case, she finally felt a flicker of real interest. "Trains speed?"

"Of course trains speed," he said. "But this one wasn't just speeding. It was going well over a hundred miles an hour."

"You know that because…?"

"I was going 70. It passed me. I had nothing else to do, so I figured out the rate of passage. Speed limits for trains on that section of track is 65. Most weeks, the trains match me, or drop back just a bit. This one was leaving me in the dust."

She was leaning forward. If the train was speeding—and if she could prove it—then the accident wasn't Ty's fault alone. He wouldn't have been able to judge how fast the train was going. And if it was going twice as fast as usual, it would have reached him two times quicker than he expected.

"So why call 911?" she asked. "What can they do?"

"Not damn thing," he said. "I just wanted it on record when the train derailed or blew through a crossing or hit some kid on the way to school."

"You could have contacted the railroad or maybe the NTSB," she said. "They could have fined the operators or pulled the engineers off the train."

"I could have," he said. "I didn't want to."

She frowned. "Why not?"

"Because I wanted the record."

And because he repeated that sentence, she felt a slight shiver. "Have you done this before? Clocked trains going too fast, I mean."

"Yeah." He sounded surprised at the question. "So?"

"Do you call 911 on people speeding in cars?"

His eyes narrowed. "No."

"So why do you call on trains?"

"I told you. The potential damage—"

"Did you contact the police after the accident, then?" she asked.

"No. It was already on record. They could find it. That attorney did."

"I wouldn't know how to compute how fast a train was going while I was driving," she said. "I mean, if we were going the same speed or something close, sure. But not an extra thirty miles an hour or more. That's quite a trick."

"Simple math," he said. "You had to do problems like that in school. We all did."

"I suppose," she said. "But it's not something I would think to do. Why did you?"

For the first time, he looked down. He didn't say anything.

"Do you have something against the railroad?" she asked.

His head shot up. "Now you sound like them."

"Them?"

"Those other lawyers."

She started to nod, but made herself stop. "What did they say?"

His lips thinned. "They said that I'm just making stuff up to get the railroad in trouble. They said that I'm pathetic. Me! I out-earn half those walking suits. I make money every damn day, and I do it without investing in any land holdings or railroad companies. They have no idea who I am."

Neither did she, really, but she thought she'd humor him.

"You're a good citizen," she said.

"Damn straight."

"Trying to protect other citizens."

"That's right."

"From the railroads."

"They think they can run all over the countryside like they're invulnerable. That train pulling oil tankers, imagine if it had derailed in that accident. You'd've heard the explosion in Rio Gordo."

Probably seen it too. He had a point.

"Tell me," she said. "Is there any way we can prove the train was going that fast?"

"The 911 call," he said.

"Besides the 911 call," she said.

He leaned back as he considered her question. "I'm sure a lot of people saw it. Or you could examine that truck. You know, it's just basic physics. If you vary the speed of an incoming train in an impact with a similar truck frame, you'll get differing results. I'm sure you can find some experts to testify."

You could find experts to testify on anything. But she didn't say that. She was curious about his expertise, though. He seemed to know a lot about trains.

She asked, "Wouldn't a train derail at that speed when it hit a truck like that?"

"Actually, no. It would be less likely to derail when it was going too fast. That truck was a cattle truck, right? If the train hit the cattle car and not the cab, then the train would've treated that truck like tissue. Most cattle cars are made of aluminum. At over a hundred miles per hour, the train would have gone through it like paper."

Interesting. She would check that.

"One last question, Mr. Williams. When did the railroad fire you?"

He blinked at her, stunned. She had caught him. That's why DRS&C's attorneys had called him pathetic. Because he had a reason for his train obsession.

A bad reason.

"That was a long time ago," he whispered.

But she still might be able to use him if he had some kind of expertise. If his old job really did require that he clock trains by sight alone.

"What did you do for them?"

He coughed, then had the grace to finally meet her gaze. "I was a security guard at the station here in Lubbock."

Security guard. Not an engineer, not anyone with special training. Just a guy with a phony badge and a gun.

"That's when you learned to clock trains," she said.

He smiled. "You have to do something to pass the time."

She bit back her frustration. For a few minutes, he'd given her some hope. But all she had was a fired security guard with a grudge.

She wrapped up the interview as politely as she could, and headed into the bright Texas sunshine.

And allowed herself one small moment to wish that C.P. Williams had been a real witness, one that could have opened this case wide.

Then she sighed, and went back to preparing her case for her jury of one.

***

MOST EVERYONE ELSE in the witness category on DRS&C's list was either a rubbernecker or someone who had made a false 911 call. Pita had had no idea how many people reported a crime or an accident *after* seeing coverage of it on television, but she was starting to learn.

She was also learning why the police didn't fine or arrest these people. Most of them were certifiably crazy.

Pita was beginning to think the list was worthless. Then she interviewed Earl Jessup Jr.

Jessup was a contractor who had been on his way to Lubbock to pick up a friend from the airport when he'd seen the accident. He'd pulled over, and because he was so well known in Rio Gordo, someone had remembered he was there.

When Pita arrived at his immaculate house in one of Rio Gordo's failed housing developments, she promised herself she wouldn't interview any more witnesses. Then Jessup pulled the door open. He smiled in recognition. So did she.

She had talked with him in the hospital cafeteria during her mother's final surgery. He'd been there for his brother, who'd been in a particularly horrendous accident, and who had somehow managed to survive.

They hadn't exchanged names.

He was a small man with brown hair in need of a good trim. His house smelled faintly of cigarette smoke and aftershave. The living room had been modified—lowered furniture, and wide paths cut through what had once been wall-to-wall carpet.

"Your brother moved in with you, huh?" she asked.

"He needed somebody," Jessup said with a finality that closed the subject.

He led her into the kitchen. On the right side of the room, the cabinets had been pulled from the walls. A dishwasher peeked out of the debris. On the left were frames for lowered countertops. Only the sink, the stove and the refrigerator remained intact, like survivors in a war zone.

He pulled a chair out for her at the kitchen table. The table was shorter than regulation height. An ashtray sat near the end of the table, but no chair. That had to be where his brother usually parked.

Pita pulled out her tape recorder and a notebook. She explained again why she was there, and asked Jessup to state some information for the record. She implied, as she had with all the others, that this informal conversation was as good as being under oath.

Jessup smiled as she went through her spiel. He seemed to know that his words would have no real bearing on the case unless he was giving a formal deposition.

"I didn't see the accident," he said. "I got there after."

He'd missed the fender benders and the first wave of the injured cows. He'd pulled up just as the train stopped. He'd been the one to organize the scene. He'd sent two men east and two men west to slow traffic until the sheriff arrived.

He'd made sure people in the various accidents exchanged insurance information, and he got the folks who'd suffered minor bumps and bruises to the side of the road. He directed a couple of teenagers to keep an eye on the injured animals, and make sure none of them made for the road again.

Then he'd headed down the embankment toward the overturned truck.

"It wasn't on fire yet?"

"No," he said. "I have no idea how it got on fire."

She frowned. "It overturned. It was leaking diesel and the engine was on."

"So the fancy Dallas lawyers tell me," he said.

"You don't believe them?"

"First thing any good driver does after an accident is shut off his engine."

"Maybe," she said. "If he's not in shock. Or seriously injured. Or both."

"Ty had enough presence of mind to make that phone call." Everyone in Rio Gordo knew about that call. Some even cursed it, thinking Nan could own the railroads if Ty hadn't picked up his cell. "He would've shut off his engine."

Pita wasn't so sure.

"Besides, he wasn't in the cab."

That caught her attention. "How do you know?"

"I saw him. He was sitting on some debris halfway up the road. That's why I was in no great hurry to get down there. He'd gotten himself out, and there wasn't much I could do until the ambulance arrived."

Jessup had a construction worker's knowledge of injuries. He knew how to treat bruises and he knew what to do for trauma. He'd talked with her about that in the cafeteria, when he'd told her how helpless he'd felt coming on his brother's car wrapped around a utility pole. He hadn't been able to get his brother out of the car—the ambulance crew later used the jaws of life—and he was afraid his brother would bleed out right there.

"But you went to help Ty anyway," Pita said.

Jessup got up, walked to the stove, and lifted up the coffee pot. He'd been brewing the old-fashioned way, in a percolator, probably because he didn't have any counter space.

"Want some?" he asked.

"Please," she said, thinking it might get him to talk.

He pulled two mugs out of the dishwasher, then set them on top of the stove. "I thought he was going to be fine."

"You're not a doctor. You don't know." She wasn't acting like a lawyer now. She was acting like a friend, and she knew it.

He grabbed the pot, and poured coffee into both mugs. Then he brought them to the table.

"I did know," he said. "I knew there was trouble, and I left."

"Sounds like you did a lot before you left," she said, trying to move him past this. She remembered long talks about his guilt over his brother's accident. "Organizing the people, making sure Ty was okay. Seems to me that you did more than most."

He shook his head.

"What else could you have done?" she asked.

"I could've gone down there and helped him," he said. "If nothing else, I could've defended him against those men with guns."

She went cold. Men with guns. She hadn't heard about men with guns.

"Who had guns?" she asked.

He gave her a self-deprecating smile, apparently realizing how dramatic he had sounded. "Everyone has guns. This is the Texas-New Mexico border."

He'd said too much, and he clearly wanted to backtrack. She wouldn't let him.

"Not everyone uses them at the scene of an accident," she said.

"If they'd've been smart, they might have. That bull was mighty scary."

"Who had guns?" she asked.

He sighed, clearly knowing she wouldn't back down. "The engineers. They carried their rifles out of the train."

She raised her eyebrows, not sure what to say.

He seemed to think she didn't believe him, so he went on. "I figured they were carrying the guns to shoot any livestock that got in their way. Made me want my gun. I'd been thinking about the accident, not a bunch of injured animals that weighed eight times what I did."

"Why did you leave?" she asked.

"It was a judgment call," he said. "I was watching those engineers walk. With purpose."

As she listened to Jessup recount the story, she realized the purpose had nothing to do with cattle. These men carried their rifles like they intended to use them. They weren't looking at the carnage. After they'd finished inspecting the train for damage, they didn't look at the train either.

Instead, they stared at Ty.

"For the entire two-mile walk?" she asked.

"I don't know," Jessup said. "That's when I decided not to stay. I thought Ty was going to be fine."

He paused. She waited, knowing if she pushed him, he might not say any more.

Jessup ran a hand through his hair. "I knew that in situations like this tempers get out of hand. I couldn't be the voice of reason. I might even get some of the blame."

He wrapped his hands around his coffee mug. He hadn't touched the liquid.

"Besides," he said, "I could see Ty's cowboys. They were riding around the train and heading toward the loose cattle near the highway. If things got ugly, they could help him. I headed back up the embankment, went to my truck, and drove on to Lubbock."

"Then I don't understand why this is bothering you," she said. "You did as much as you could, and then you left it to others, the ones who needed to handle the problem."

"Yeah," he said softly. "I tell myself that."

"But?"

He tilted his head, as if shaking some thoughts loose. "But a couple of things don't make sense. Like why did Ty go back into the cab of that truck? And how come no one smelled the diesel? Wouldn't it bother them so close to the oil tankers?"

She waited, watching him. He shrugged.

"And then there's the nightmares."

"Nightmares?" she asked.

"I get into my truck, and as I slam the door, I hear a gunshot. It's half a second behind the sound of the door slamming, but it's clear."

"Did you really hear that?" she asked.

"I like to think if I did, I would've gone back. But I didn't. I just drove away, like nothing had happened. And a friend of mine died."

He didn't say anything else. She took another sip of her coffee, careful not to set the mug to close to her recorder.

"No one else reported gunshots," she said.

He nodded.

"No one else saw Ty outside that cab," she said.

"He was in a gully. I was the only one who went down the embankment. You couldn't see him from the road."

"And the truck? Could you see it?"

He shook his head.

"What do you think happened?" she asked.

"I don't know," he said, "and it's driving me insane."

***

It bothered her too, but not in quite the same way.

She found Jessup in DRS&C's list of 911 nutcases. He'd been buried among the crazies, just like important information was probably hidden in the boxes that littered her office floor.

No one else had seen the angry engineers or Ty out of the truck, but no one could quite figure out how he'd made that cell phone call either. If he'd been sitting on some debris outside the cab, that made more sense than calling from inside, while bleeding, with the engine running and diesel dripping.

But Jessup was right. It raised some disturbing questions.

They bothered her, enough so that she called Nan on her cell phone during the drive back to her office.

"Do you have a copy of the autopsy report for Ty?" Pita asked.

"There was no autopsy," Nan said. "It's pretty clear how he died."

Pita sighed. "What about the truck? What happened to it?"

"Last I saw, it was in Digger's Salvage Yard."

So Pita pulled into the salvage yard, and parked near a dented Toyota. Digger was a good ole boy who salvaged parts, and when he couldn't, he used a crusher to demolish the vehicles into metal for scrap.

But he still had the cab of that truck—insurance wouldn't release it until the case was settled.

For the first time, she looked at the cab herself, but couldn't see anything except charred metal, a steel frame, and a ruined interior. She wasn't an expert, and she needed one.

It took only a moment to call an old friend in Albuquerque who knew a good freelance forensic examiner. The examiner wanted $500 plus expenses to travel to Rio Gordo and look at the truck.

Pita hesitated. She could've—and should've—called Nan for the expense money.

But the examiner's presence would raise Nan's hopes. And right now, Pita couldn't do that. She was trusting a man she'd met late night at the hospital, a man who talked her through her mother's last illness, a man she couldn't quite get enough distance from to examine his veracity.

She needed more than Jessup's nightmares and speculations. She needed something that might pass for proof.

***

"I CAN'T TELL YOU when it got there," said the examiner, Walter Shepard. He was a slender man with intense eyes. He wore a plaid shirt despite the heat and tan trousers that had pilled from too many washings.

He was sitting in Pita's office. She had moved some boxes aside so that the path into the office was wider. She'd also found a chair that had been buried since the case began.

He pushed some photographs onto her desk. The photographs were close-ups of the truck's cab. He'd thoughtfully drawn an arrow next to the tiny hole in the door on the driver's side.

"It's definitely a bullet hole. It's too smooth to be anything else," he said. "And there's another in the seat. I was able to recover part of a bullet."

He shifted the photos so that she could see a shattered metal fragment.

"The problem is I can't tell you anything else, except that the bullet holes predate the fire. I can't tell you how long they were there or how they got there. They could be real old. Or brand new. I can't tell."

"That's all right." A bullet hole, along with Jessup's testimony, was enough to cast doubt on everything. She felt like she could go to DRS&C and ask for a settlement.

She wasn't even regretting that she hadn't worked on contingency. This case was proving easier than she had thought it would be.

"I know you asked me to look for evidence of shooting or a fight," Shepard said, "but I wouldn't be doing my job if I let it go at that. The anomaly here isn't the bullets. It's the fire itself."

She looked up from the photos, surprised. Shepard wasn't watching her. He was still studying the photographs. He put a finger on one of them.

"The diesel leaked. There's runoff along the tank and a drip pattern that trails to the passenger side of the cab."

The cab had landed on its passenger side.

"But the fire started here." He was touching the photo of the interior of the cab. He pushed his finger against the image of the ruined seat. "See how the flames spread upwards. You can see the burn pattern. And fuel fed it. It burned around something—probably the body—so it looks to me like someone poured fuel onto the body itself and lit it on fire. I didn't find a match, but I found the remains of a Bic lighter on the floor of the cab. It melted but it's not burned the way everything else is. I think it was tossed in after the fire started."

Pita was having trouble wrapping her mind around what he was saying. "You're saying someone deliberately started the fire? So close to oil tankers?"

"I think that someone knew the truck wouldn't explode. The fire was pretty contained."

"Some people from the highway had a fire extinguisher in their car. It was too late to save Ty."

"You'll want your examiner to look at the body again," Shepard said. "I have a hunch you'll find that your client's husband was dead before he burned, not after."

"Based on this pattern."

"A man doesn't sit calmly and let himself burn to death," Shepard said. "He was able to make a phone call. He was conscious. He would have tried to get out of that cab. He didn't."

Pita was shaking. If this was true, then this case went way beyond a simple accident. If this was true, then those engineers shot Ty and tried to cover it up.

Ballsy, considering how close to the road they had been.

But the other drivers had been preoccupied with their own accidents and the injured cows and stopping traffic. No one except Jessup had even tried to come down the embankment.

And the engineers, who drove the route a lot, would have known how hard that truck was to see from the road.

They would have figured that the burning cab would get put out once someone saw the smoke. No wonder they'd lit the body. They didn't want to risk catching the cab on fire, and leaving the bullet-ridden corpse untouched.

"You're sure?" Pita asked.

"Positive." Shepard gathered the photos. "If I were you, I'd take this to the state police. You don't have an accident here. You have cold-blooded murder."

***

THE NEXT FEW WEEKS became a blur. DRS&C dropped the suit, becoming the friendliest big law firm that Pita had ever known. Which made her wonder when they'd realized that the engineers had committed murder.

Either way, it didn't matter. DRS&C was willing to work with her, to do whatever it took to "make Mrs. Hughes happy."

Nan wouldn't be happy until her husband's killers were brought to justice. She snapped into action the moment the state coroner confirmed Shepard's hunches. Ty had been shot in the skull before he died, and then his body had been burned to cover up the crime.

If Nan hadn't worked so hard and believed in her husband so much, no one would have known.

The story came out slowly. The train had been speeding when Ty crossed the tracks. Williams' estimate of more than 100 miles per hour was probably correct—enough for the railroads to have liability right there.

But the engineers, both frightened by the accident itself and terrified for their jobs, had walked the length of the train to Ty's overturned truck and, finding him alive and relatively unhurt, let their anger explode.

They'd threatened him with the loss of everything if he didn't confess that he had failed to beat the train. He'd made the call to satisfy them. But it hadn't worked. Somehow—and neither man was going to admit how (not even more than a year later at sentencing)—one of the rifles had gone off, killing him. Then they'd stuffed him in the cab—whose ignition was off—poured some diesel from the spill on him, and lit him on fire.

They watched him burn for a few minutes before going up the embankment to see if anyone had a fire extinguisher in his car. Fortunately someone did. Otherwise, they planned to have someone drive them the two miles to the engine for the train's fire extinguishers.

The engineers were eventually convicted, Nan got to keep her ranch and her husband's reputation, and the railroads kept trying to settle.

But Pita insisted that Nan hire an attorney who specialized in cases against big companies. Pita helped with the hire, finding someone with a great reputation who wasn't afraid of a thousand boxes of evidence and, more importantly, would work on contingency.

"You sure you don't want it?" Nan had asked, maybe two dozen times.

And each time, Pita had said, "Positive. The case is too big for me."

Although it wasn't. She could have gone to La Jolla, Webster, and Garcia as a rainmaker, someone who brought in a huge case and made millions for the company.

But she didn't.

Because this case had taught her a few things.

She'd learned that she hated big cases with lots and lots of evidence.

She'd learned that she really didn't care about the money. (Although the ten thousand dollar bonus that Nan had paid her—a bonus Pita hadn't asked for—had come in very handy.)

And she learned how valuable it was to know the people of her town. If she hadn't spent all those evenings in the cafeteria with Jessup, she wouldn't have trusted his story, and she never would have hired the forensic examiner.

Her mom had been right, all those years ago. Rio Gordo wasn't a bad place. Yeah, it was impoverished. Yeah, it was filled with dust, and didn't have a good nightlife or a great university.

But it did have some pretty spectacular people.

People who congratulated Pita for the next year on her success in the Hughes case. People who now came to her to do their wills or their prenups. People who asked her advice on the smallest legal matters, and believed her when she gave them an unvarnished opinion.

Her biggest case had helped her discover her calling: She was a small town attorney—someone who cared more about the people around her than the money their cases could bring in.

She wouldn't be rich.

But she would be happy.

And that was more than enough.

Cowboy Grace

"Every woman tolerates misogyny." Alex said. She slid her empty beer glass across the bar, and tucked a strand of her auburn hair behind her ear. "How much depends on how old she is. The older she is the less she notices it. The more she expects it."

"Bullshit." Carole took a drag on her Virginia Slim, crossed her legs, and adjusted her skirt. "I don't tolerate misogyny."

"Maybe we should define the word," Grace said, moving to the other side of Carole. She wished her friend would realize how much the smoking irritated her. In fact, the entire night was beginning to irritate her. They were all avoiding the topic du jour: the tiny wound on Grace's left breast, stitches gone now, but the skin still raw and sore.

"Mis-ah-jenny." Carole said, as if Grace were stupid. "Hatred of women."

"From the Greek," Alex said. "Misos or hatred and gyne or women."

"Not," Carole said, waving her cigarette as if it were a baton, "misogamy, which is also from the Greek. Hatred of marriage. Hmm. Two male misos wrapped in one."

The bartender, a diminutive woman dressed wearing a red and white cowgirl outfit, complete with fringe and gold buttons, snickered. She set down a napkin in front of Alex and gave her another beer.

"Compliments," she said, "of the men at the booth near the phone."

Alex looked. She always looked. She was tall, busty, and leggy, with a crooked nose thanks to an errant pitch Grace had thrown in the 9th grade, a long chin and eyes the color of wine. Men couldn't get enough of her. When Alex rebuffed them, they slept with Carole and then talked to Grace.

The men in the booth near the phone looked like corporate types on a junket. Matching gray suits, different ties—all in a complimentary shade of pink, red, or cranberry—matching haircuts (long on top, styled on the sides), and differing goofy grins.

"This is a girl bar," Alex said, shoving the glass back at the bartender. "We come here to diss men, not to meet them."

"Good call," Carole said, exhaling smoke into Grace's face. Grace agreed, not with the smoke or the rejection, but because she wanted time with her friends. Without male intervention of any kind.

"Maybe we should take a table," Grace said.

"Maybe." Carole crossed her legs again. Her mini was leather, which meant that night she felt like being on display. "Or maybe we should send drinks to the cutest men we see."

They scanned the bar. Happy Hour at the Oh Kaye Corral didn't change much from Friday to Friday. A jukebox in the corner, playing Patty Loveless. Cocktail waitresses in short skirts and ankle boots with big heels. Tin stars and Wild West art on the walls, unstained wood and checkered tablecloths adding to the effect. One day, when Grace had Alex's courage and Carole's gravely voice, she wanted to walk in, belly up to the bar, slap her hand on its polished surface, and order whiskey straight up. She wanted someone to challenge her. She wanted to pull her six-gun and have a stare-down, then and there. Cowboy Grace, fastest gun in the West. Or at least in Racine on a rainy Friday night.

"I don't see cute," Alex said. "I see married, married, divorced, desperate, single, single, never-been-laid, and married."

Grace watched her make her assessment. Alex's expression never changed. Carole was looking at the men, apparently seeing whether or not she agreed.

Typically, she didn't.

"I dunno," she said, pulling on her cigarette. "Never-Been-Laid's kinda cute."

"So try him," Alex said. "But you'll have your own faithful puppy dog by this time next week, and a proposal of marriage within the month."

Carole grinned and slid off the stool. "Proposal of marriage in two weeks," she said. "I'm that good."

She stubbed out her cigarette, grabbed the tiny leather purse that matched the skirt, adjusted her silk blouse and sashayed her way toward a table in the middle.

Grace finally saw Never-Been-Laid. He had soft brown eyes, and hair that needed trimming. He wore a shirt that accented his narrow shoulders, and he had a laptop open on the round table. He was alone. He had his feet tucked under the chair, crossed at the ankles. He wore dirty tennis shoes with his Gap khakis.

"Cute?" Grace said.

"Shhh," Alex said. "It's a door into the mind of Carole."

"One that should remain closed." Grace moved to Carole's stool. It was still warm. Grace shoved Carole's drink out of her way, grabbed her glass of wine, and coughed. The air still smelled of cigarette smoke.

Carole was leaning over the extra chair, giving Never-Been-Laid a view of her cleavage, and the guys at the booth by the phone a nice look at her ass, which they seemed to appreciate.

"Where the hell did that misogyny comment come from?" Grace asked.

Alex looked at her. "You want to get a booth?"

"Sure. Think Carole can find us?"

"I think Carole's going to be deflowering a computer geek and not caring what we're doing." Alex grabbed her drink, stood, and walked to a booth on the other side of the Corral. Dirty glasses from the last occupants were piled in the center, and the red-and-white checked vinyl tablecloth was sticky.

They moved the glasses on the edge of the table and didn't touch the dollar tip, which had been pressed into a puddle of beer.

Grace set her wine down and slid onto her side. Alex did the same on the other side. Somehow they managed not to touch the tabletop at all.

"You remember my boss?" Alex asked as she adjusted the tiny fake gas lamp that hung on the wall beside the booth.

"Beanie Boy?"

She grinned. "Yeah."

"Never met him."

"Aren't you lucky."

Grace already knew that. She'd heard stories about Beanie Boy for the last year. They had started shortly after he was hired. Alex went to the company Halloween party and was startled to find her boss dressed as one of the Lollipop Kids from the Wizard of Oz, complete with striped shirt, oversized lollipop and propeller beanie.

"Now what did he do?" Grace asked.

"Called me honey."

"Yeah?" Grace asked.

"And sweetie, and doll-face, and sugar."

"Hasn't he been doing that for the last year?"

Alex glared at Grace. "It's getting worse."

"What's he doing, patting you on the butt?"

"If he did, I'd get him for harassment, and he knows it."

She had lowered her voice. Grace could barely hear her over Shania Twain.

"This morning one of our clients came in praising the last report. I wrote it."

"Didn't Beanie Boy give you credit?"

"Of course he did. He said, 'Our little Miss Rogers wrote it. Isn't she a doll?'"

Grace clutched her drink tighter. This didn't matter to her. Her biopsy was benign. She had called Alex and Carole and told them. They'd suggested coming here. So why weren't they offering a toast to her life? Why weren't they celebrating, really celebrating, instead of rerunning the same old conversation in the same old bar in the same old way? "What did the client do?"

"He agreed, of course."

"And?"

"And what?"

"Is that it? Didn't you speak up?"

"How could I? He was praising me, for godssake."

Grace sighed and sipped her beer. Shania Twain's comment was that didn't impress her much. It didn't impress Grace much either, but she knew better than to say anything to Alex.

Grace looked toward the middle of the restaurant. Carole was standing behind Never-Been-Laid, her breasts pressed against his back, her ass on view to the world, her head over his shoulder peering at his computer screen.

Alex didn't follow her gaze like Grace had hoped. "If I were ten years younger, I'd tell Beanie Boy to shove it."

"If you were ten years younger, you wouldn't have a mortgage and a Mazda."

"Dignity shouldn't be cheaper than a paycheck," she said.

"So confront him."

"He doesn't think he's doing anything wrong. He treats all the women like that."

Grace sighed. They'd walked this road before. Job after job, boyfriend after boyfriend. Alex, for all her looks, was like Joe McCarthy protecting the world from the Red Menace: she saw anti-female everywhere, and most of it, she was convinced, was directed at her.

"You don't seem very sympathetic," Alex said.

She wasn't. She never had been. And with all she had been through in the last month, *alone* because her two best friends couldn't bear to talk about the Big C, the lock that was usually on Grace's mouth wasn't working.

"I'm not sympathetic," Grace said. "I'm beginning to think you're a victim in search of a victimizer."

"That's not fair, Grace," Alex said. "We tolerate this stuff because we were raised in an anti-woman society. It's gotten better, but it's not perfect. You tell those Xers stuff like this and they shake their heads. Or the new ones. What're they calling themselves now? Generation Y? They were raised on Title IX. Hell, they pull off their shirts after winning soccer games. Imagine us doing that."

"My cousin got arrested in 1977 in Milwaukee on the day Elvis Presley died for playing volleyball," Grace said. Carole was actually rubbing herself on Never-Been-Laid. His face was the color of the red checks in the tablecloth.

"What?"

Grace turned to Alex. "My cousin. You know, Barbie? She got arrested playing volleyball."

"They didn't let girls play volleyball in Milwaukee?"

"It was 90 degrees, and she was playing with a group of guys. They pulled off their shirts because they were hot and sweating, so she did the same. She got arrested for indecent exposure."

"God," Alex said. "Did she go to jail?"

"Didn't even get her day in court."

"Everyone gets a day in court."

Grace shook her head. "The judge took one look at Barbie, who was really butch in those days, and said, 'I'm sick of you girls coming in here and arguing that you should have equal treatment for things that are clearly unequal. I do not establish Public Decency laws. You may show a bit of breast if you're feeding a child, otherwise you are in violation of—some damn code.' Barbie used to quote the thing chapter and verse."

"Then what?" Alex asked.

"Then she got married, had a kid, and started wearing nail polish. She said it wasn't as much fun to show her breasts legally."

"See?" Alex said. "Misogyny."

Grace shrugged. "Society, Alex. Get used to it."

"That's the point of your story? We've been oppressed for a thousand years and you say, 'Get used to it'?"

"I say Brandi Chastain pulls off her shirt in front of millions—"

"Showing a sports bra."

"—and she doesn't get arrested. I say women head companies all the time. I say things are better now than they were when I was growing up, and I say the only ones who oppress us are ourselves."

"I say you're drunk."

Grace pointed at Carole, who was wet-kissing Never-Been-Laid, her arms wrapped around his neck and her legs wrapped around his waist. "She's drunk. I'm just speaking out."

"You never speak out."

Grace sighed. No one had picked up the glasses and she was tired of looking at that poor drowning dollar bill. There wasn't going to be any celebration. Everything was the same as it always was—at least to Alex and Carole. But Grace wanted something different.

She got up, threw a five next to the dollar, and picked up her purse.

"Tell me if Carole gets laid," Grace said, and left.

Outside Grace stopped and took a deep breath of the humid, exhaust-filled air. She could hear the clang of glasses even in the parking lot and the rhythm of Mary Chapin Carpenter praising passionate kisses. Grace had had only one glass of wine and a lousy time, and she wondered why people said old friends were the best friends. They were supposed to raise toasts to her future, now restored. She'd even said the "b" word and Alex hadn't noticed. It was as if the cancer scare had happened to someone they didn't even know.

Grace was going to be forty years old in three weeks. Her two best friends were probably planning a version of the same party they had held for her when she turned thirty. A male stripper whose sweaty body repulsed her more than aroused her, too many black balloons, and aging jokes that hadn't been original the first time around.

Forty years old, an accountant with her own firm, no close family, no boyfriend, and a resident of the same town her whole life. The only time she left was to visit cousins out east, and for what? Obligation?

There was no joy left, if there'd ever been any joy at all.

She got into her sensible Ford Taurus, bought at a used car lot for well under Blue Book, and drove west.

***

It wasn't until she reached Janesville that she started to call herself crazy, and it wasn't until she drove into Dubuque that she realized how little tied her to her hometown.

An apartment without even a cat to cozy up to, a business no more successful than a dozen others, and people who still saw her as a teenager wearing granny glasses, braces and hair too long for her face. Grace, who was always there. Grace the steady, Grace the smart. Grace, who helped her friends out of their financial binds, who gave them a shoulder to cry on, and a degree of comfort because their lives weren't as empty as her own.

When she had told Alex and Carole that her mammogram had come back suspicious, they had looked away. When she told them that she had found a lump, they had looked frightened.

I can't imagine life without you, Gracie, Carole had whispered.

Imagine it now, Grace thought.

The dawn was breaking when she reached Cedar Rapids, and she wasn't really tired. But she was practical, had always been practical, and habits of a lifetime didn't change just because she had run away from home at the age of 39.

She got a hotel room and slept for eight hours, got up, had dinner in a nice steak place, went back to the room and slept some more. When she woke up Sunday morning to bells from the Presbyterian Church across the street, she lay on her back and listened for a good minute before she realized they were playing "What a Friend We Have in Jesus." And she smiled then, because Jesus had been a better friend to her in recent years than Alex and Carole ever had.

At least Jesus didn't tell her his problems when she was praying about hers. If Jesus was self-absorbed he wasn't obvious about it. And he didn't seem to care that she hadn't been inside a church since August of 1978.

The room was chintz, the wallpaper and the bedspread matched, and the painting on the wall was chosen for its color not for its technique. Grace sat up and wondered what she was doing here, and thought about going home.

To nothing.

So she got in her car and followed the Interstate, through Des Moines, and Lincoln and Cheyenne, places she had only read about, places she had never seen. How could a woman live for forty years and not see the country of her birth? How could a woman do nothing except what she was supposed to from the day she was born until the day she died?

In Salt Lake City, she stared at the Mormon Tabernacle, all white against an azure sky. She sat in her car and watched a groundskeeper maintain the flowers, and remembered how it felt to take her doctor's call.

A lot of women have irregular mammograms, particularly at your age. The breast tissue is thicker, and often we get clouds.

Clouds.

There were fluffy clouds in the dry desert sky, but they were white and benign. Just like her lump had turned out to be. But for a hellish month, she had thought about that lump, feeling it when she woke out of a sound sleep, wondering if it presaged the beginning of the end. She had never felt her mortality like this before, not even when her mother, the only parent she had known, had died. Not even when she realized there was no one remaining of the generation that had once stood between her and death.

No one talked about these things. No one let her talk about them either. Not just Alex and Carole, but Michael, her second-in-command at work, or even her doctor, who kept assuring her that she was young and the odds were in her favor.

Young didn't matter if the cancer had spread through the lymph nodes. When she went in for the lumpectomy almost two weeks ago now, she had felt a curious kind of relief, as if the doctor had removed a tick that had burrowed under her skin. When he had called with the news that the lump was benign, she had thanked him calmly and continued with her day, filing corporate tax returns for a consulting firm.

No one had known the way she felt. Not relieved. No. It was more like she had received a reprieve.

The clouds above the Tabernacle helped calm her. She plugged in her cell phone for the first time in days and listened to the voice mail messages, most of them from Michael, growing increasingly worried about where she was.

Have you forgotten the meeting with Boyd's? he'd asked on Monday.

Do you want me to file Charlie's extension? he'd demanded on Tuesday.

Where the hell are you? he cried on Wednesday and she knew, then, that it was okay to call him, that not even the business could bring her home.

Amazing how her training had prepared her for moments like these and she hadn't even known it. She had savings, lots of them, because she hadn't bought a house even though it had been prudent to do so. She had been waiting, apparently, for Mr. Right, or the family her mother had always wanted for her, the family that would never come. Her money was invested properly, and she could live off the interest if she so chose. She had just never chosen to before.

And if she didn't want to be found, she didn't have to be. She knew how to have the interest paid through offshore accounts so that no one could track it. She even knew a quick and almost legal way to change her name. Traceable, but she hadn't committed a crime. She didn't need to hide well, just well enough that a casual search wouldn't produce her.

Not that anyone would start a casual search. Once she sold the business, Michael would forget her and Alex and Carole, even though they would gossip about her at Oh Kaye's every Friday night for the rest of their lives, wouldn't summon the energy to search.

She could almost hear them now: *She met some guy*, Carole would say. *And he killed her,* Alex would add, and then they would argue until last call, unless Carole found some man to entertain her, and Alex someone else to complain to. They would miss Grace only when they screwed up, when they needed a shoulder, when they couldn't stand being on their own. And even then, they probably wouldn't realize what it was they had lost.

***

BECAUSE IT AMUSED HER, she had driven north to Boise, land of the white collar, to make her cell call to Michael. Her offer to him was simple: cash her out of the business and call it his own. She named a price, he dickered half-heartedly, she refused to negotiate. Within two days, he had wired the money to a blind money market account that she had often stored cash in for the firm.

She let the money sit there while she decided what to do with it. Then she went to Reno to change her name.

Reno had been a surprise. A beautiful city set between mountains like none she had ever seen. The air was dry, the downtown tacky, the people friendly. There were bookstores and slot machines and good restaurants. There were cheap houses and all-night casinos and lots of strange places. There was even history, of the Wild West kind.

For the first time in her life, Grace fell in love.

And to celebrate the occasion, she snuck into a quickie wedding chapel, found the marriage licenses, took one, copied down the name of the chapel, its permit number, and all the other pertinent information, and then returned to her car. There she checked the boxes, saying she had seen the driver's licenses and birth certificates of the people involved, including a fictitious man named Nathan Reinhart, and *viola!* she was married. She had a new name, a document the credit card companies would accept, and a new beginning all at the same time.

***

Using some of her personal savings, she bought a house with lots of windows and a view of the Sierras. In the mornings, light bathed her kitchen, and in the evenings, it caressed her living room. She had never seen light like this—clean and pure and crisp. She was beginning to understand why artists moved west to paint, why people used to exclaim about the way light changed everything.

The lack of humidity, of dense air pollution, made the air clearer. The elevation brought her closer to the sun.

She felt as if she were seeing everything for the very first time.

And hearing it, too. The house was silent, much more silent than an apartment, and the silence soothed her. She could listen to her television without worrying about the people in the apartment below, or play her stereo full blast without concern about a visit from the super.

There was a freedom to having her own space that she hadn't realized before, a freedom to living the way she wanted to live, without the rules of the past or the expectations she had grown up with.

And among those expectations was the idea that she had to be the strong one, the good one, the one on whose shoulder everyone else cried. She had no friends here, no one who needed her shoulder, and she had no one who expected her to be good.

Only herself.

Of course, in some things she was good. Habits of a lifetime died hard. She began researching the best way to invest Michael's lump sum payment—and while she researched, she left the money alone. She kept her house clean and her lawn, such as it was in this high desert, immaculate. She got a new car and made sure it was spotless.

No one would find fault with her appearances, inside or out.

Not that she had anyone who was looking. She didn't have a boyfriend or a job or a hobby. She didn't have anything except herself.

***

SHE FOUND HERSELF drawn to the casinos, with their clinking slot machines, musical come-ons, and bright lights. No matter how high tech the places had become, no matter how clean, how "family-oriented," they still had a shady feel.

Or perhaps that was her upbringing, in a state where gambling had been illegal until she was 25, a state where her father used to play a friendly game of poker—even with his friends—with the curtains drawn.

Sin—no matter how sanitized—still had appeal in the brand-new century.

Of course, she was too sensible to gamble away her savings. The slots lost their appeal quickly, and when she sat down at the blackjack tables, she couldn't get past the feeling that she was frittering her money away for nothing.

But she liked the way the cards fell and how people concentrated—as if their very lives depended on this place—and she was good with numbers. One of the pit bosses mentioned that they were always short of poker dealers, so she took a class offered by one of the casinos. Within two months, she was snapping cards, raking pots, and wearing a uniform that made her feel like Carole on a bad night.

It only took a few weeks for her bosses to realize that Grace was a natural poker dealer. They gave her the busy shifts—Thursday through Sunday nights—and she spent her evenings playing the game of cowboys, fancy men, and whores. Finally, there was a bit of an Old West feel to her life, a bit of excitement, a sense of purpose.

When she got off at midnight, she would be too keyed up to go home. She started bringing a change of clothes to work and, after her shift, she would go to the casino next door. It had a great bar upstairs—filled with brass, Victorian furnishings, and a real hardwood floor. She could get a sandwich and a beer. Finally, she felt like she was becoming the woman she wanted to be.

One night, a year after she had run away from home, a man sidled up next to her. He had long blond hair that curled against his shoulders. His face was tanned and lined, a bit too thin. He looked road-hardened—like a man who'd been outside too much, seen too much, worked in the sun too much. His hands were long, slender, and callused. He wore no rings, and his shirt cuffs were frayed at the edges.

He sat beside her in companionable silence for nearly an hour, while they both stared at CNN on the big screen over the bar, and then he said, "Just once I'd like to go someplace authentic."

His voice was cigarette growly, even though he didn't smoke, and he had a Southern accent that was soft as butter. She guessed Louisiana, but it might have been Tennessee or even Northern Florida. She wasn't good at distinguishing Southern accents yet. She figured she would after another year or so of dealing cards.

"You should go up to Virginia City. There's a bar or two that looks real enough."

He snorted through his nose. "Tourist trap."

She shrugged. She'd thought it interesting—an entire historic city, preserved just like it had been when Mark Twain lived there. "Seems to me if you weren't a tourist there wouldn't be any other reason to go."

He shrugged and picked up a toothpick, rolling it in his fingers. She smiled to herself. A former smoker then, and a fidgeter.

"Reno's better than Vegas, at least," he said. "Casinos aren't family friendly yet."

"Except Circus Circus."

"Always been that way. But the rest. You get a sense that maybe it ain't all legal here."

She looked at him sideways. He was at least her age, his blue eyes sharp in his leathery face. "You like things that aren't legal?"

"Gambling's not something that should be made pretty, you know? It's about money, and money can either make you or destroy you."

She felt herself smile, remember what it was like to paw through receipts and tax returns, to make neat rows of figures about other people's money. "What's the saying?" she asked. "Money is like sex—"

"It doesn't matter unless you don't have any." To her surprise, he laughed. The sound was rich and warm, not at all like she had expected. The smile transformed his face into something almost handsome.

He tapped the toothpick on the polished bar, and asked, "You think that's true?"

She shrugged. "I suppose. Everyone's idea of what's enough differs, though."

"What's yours?" He turned toward her, smile gone now, eyes even sharper than they had been a moment ago. She suddenly felt as if she were on trial.

"My idea of what's enough?" she asked.

He nodded.

"I suppose enough that I can live off the interest in the manner in which I've become accustomed. What's yours?"

A shadow crossed his eyes and he looked away from her. "Long as I've got a roof over my head, clothes on my back, and food in my mouth, I figure I'm rich enough."

"Sounds distinctly unAmerican to me," she said.

He looked at her sideways again. "I guess it does, don't it? Women figure a man should have some sort of ambition."

"Do you?"

"Have ambition?" He bent the toothpick between his fore- and middle fingers. "Of course I do. It just ain't tied in with money, is all."

"I thought money and ambition went together."

"In most men's minds."

"But not yours?"

The toothpick broke. "Not any more," he said.

***

THREE NIGHTS LATER, he sat down at her table. He was wearing a denim shirt with silver snaps and jeans so faded that they looked as if they might shred around him. That, his hair, and his lean look reminded Grace of a movie gunslinger, the kind that cleaned a town up because it had to be done.

"Guess you don't make enough to live off the interest," he said to her as he sat down.

She raised her eyebrows. "Maybe I like people."

"Maybe you like games."

She smiled and dealt the cards. The table was full. She was dealing 3-6 Texas Hold 'Em and most of the players were locals. It was Monday night and they all looked pleased to have an unfamiliar face at the table.

If she had known him better she might have tipped him off. Instead she wanted to see how long his money would last.

He bought in for $100, although she had seen at least five hundred in his wallet. He took the chips, and studied them for a moment.

He had three tells. He fidgeted with his chips when his cards were mediocre and he was thinking of bluffing. He bit his lower lip when he had nothing, and his eyes went dead flat when he had a winning hand.

He lost the first hundred in forty-five minutes, bought back in for another hundred and managed to hold onto it until her shift ended shortly after midnight. He sat through dealer changes and the floating fortunes of his cards. When she returned from her last break, she found herself wondering if his tells were subconscious after all. They seemed deliberately calculated to let the professional poker players around him think that he was a rookie.

She said nothing. She couldn't, really—at least not overtly. The casino got a rake and they didn't allow her to do anything except deal the game. She had no stake in it anyway. She hadn't lied to him that first night. She loved watching people, the way they played their hands, the way the money flowed.

It was like being an accountant, only in real time. She got to see the furrowed brows as the decisions were made, hear the curses as someone pushed back a chair and tossed in that last hand of cards, watch the desperation that often led to the exact wrong play. Only as a poker dealer, she wasn't required to clean up the mess. She didn't have to offer advice or refuse it; she didn't have to worry about tax consequences, about sitting across from someone else's auditor, justifying choices she had no part in making.

When she got off, she changed into her tightest jeans and a summer sweater and went to her favorite bar.

Casino bars were always busy after midnight, even on a Monday. The crowd wasn't there to have a good time but to wind down from one—or to prepare itself for another.

She sat at the bar, as she had since she started this routine, and she'd been about to leave when he sat next to her.

"Lose your stake?" she asked.

"I'm up $400."

She looked at him sideways. He didn't seem pleased with the way the night had gone—not the way a casual player would have been. Her gut instinct was right. He was someone who was used to gambling—and winning.

"Buy you another?" he asked.

She shook her head. "One's enough."

He smiled. It made him look less fierce and gave him a rugged sort of appeal. "Everything in moderation?"

"Not always," she said. "At least, not any more."

***

Somehow they ended up in bed—her bed—and he was better than she imagined his kind of man could be. He had knowledgeable fingers and endless patience. He didn't seem to mind the scar on her breast. Instead he lingered over it, focusing on it as if it were an erogenous zone. His pleasure at the result enhanced hers and when she finally fell asleep, somewhere around dawn, she was more sated than she had ever been.

She awoke to the smell of frying bacon and fresh coffee. Her eyes were filled with sand, but her body had a healthy lethargy.

At least, she thought, *he hadn't left before she awoke.*

At least he hadn't stolen everything in sight.

She still didn't know his name, and wasn't sure she cared. She slipped on a robe and combed her hair with her fingers and walked into her kitchen—the kitchen no one had cooked in but her.

He had on his denims and his hair was tied back with a leather thong. He had found not only her cast iron skillet but the grease cover that she always used when making bacon. A bowl of scrambled eggs steamed on the counter, and a plate of heavily buttered toast sat beside it.

"Sit down, darlin'," he said. "Let me bring it all to you."

She flushed. That was what it felt like he had done the night before, but she said nothing. Her juice glasses were out, and so was her everyday ware, and yet somehow the table looked like it had been set for a *Gourmet* photo spread.

"I certainly didn't expect this," she said.

"It's the least I can do." He put the eggs and toast on the table, then poured her a cup of coffee. Cream and sugar were already out, and in their special containers.

She was slightly uncomfortable that he had figured out her kitchen that quickly and well.

He put the bacon on a paper-towel covered plate, then set that on the table. She hadn't moved, so he beckoned with his hand.

"Go ahead," he said. "It's getting cold."

He sat across from her and helped himself to bacon while she served herself eggs. They were fluffy and light, just like they would have been in a restaurant. She had no idea how he got that consistency. Her home-scrambled eggs were always runny and undercooked.

The morning light bathed the table, giving everything a bright glow. His hair seemed even blonder in the sunlight and his skin darker. He had laugh lines around his mouth, and a bit of blond stubble on his chin.

She watched him eat, those nimble fingers scooping up the remaining egg with a slice of toast, and found herself remembering how those fingers had felt on her skin.

Then she felt his gaze on her, and looked up. His eyes were dead flat for just an instant, and she felt herself grow cold.

"Awful nice house," he said slowly, "for a woman who makes a living dealing cards."

Her first reaction was defense—she wanted to tell him she had other income, and what did he care about a woman who dealt cards, anyway?—but instead, she smiled. "Thank you."

He measured her, as if he expected a different response, then he said, "You're awfully calm considering that you don't even know my name. You don't strike me as the kind of woman who does this often."

His words startled her, but she made sure that the surprise didn't show. She had learned a lot about her own tells while dealing poker, and the experience was coming in handy now.

"You flatter yourself," she said softly.

"Well," he said, reaching into his back pocket, "if there's one thing my job's taught me, it's that people hide information they don't want anyone else to know."

He pulled out his wallet, opened it, and with two fingers removed a business card. He dropped it on the table.

She didn't want to pick the card up. She knew things had already changed between them in a way she didn't entirely understand, but she had a sense from the fleeting expression she had seen on his face that once she picked up the card she could never go back.

She set down her coffee cup and used two fingers to slide the card toward her. It identified him as Travis Delamore, a skip tracer and bail bondsman. Below his name was a phone number with a 414 exchange.

Milwaukee, Wisconsin and the surrounding areas. Precisely the place someone from Racine might call if they wanted to hire a professional.

She slipped the card into the pocket of her robe. "Is sleeping around part of your job?"

"Is embezzling part of yours?" All the warmth had left his face. His expression was unreadable except for the flatness in his eyes. What did he think he knew?

She made herself smile. "Mr. Delamore, if I stole a dime from the casino, I'd be instantly fired. There are cameras everywhere."

"I mean your former job, Ms. Mackie. A lot of money is missing from your office."

"I don't have an office." His use of her former name made her hands clammy. What had Michael done?

"Do you deny that you're Grace Mackie?"

"I don't acknowledge or deny anything. When did this become an inquisition, Mr. Delamore? I thought men liked their sex uncomplicated. You seem to be a unique member of your species."

This time he smiled. "Of course we like our sex uncomplicated. That's why we're having this discussion this morning."

"If we'd had it last night, there wouldn't be a this morning."

"That's my point." He downed the last of his orange juice. "And thank you for the acknowledgement, Ms. Mackie."

"It wasn't an acknowledgement," she said. "I don't like to sleep with men who think me guilty of something."

"Embezzlement," he said gently, using the same tone he had used in bed. This time, it made her bristle.

"I haven't stolen anything."

"New house, new name, new town, mysterious disappearance."

The chill she had felt earlier grew. She stood and wrapped her robe tightly around her waist. "I don't know what you think you know, Mr. Delamore, but I believe it's time for you to leave."

He didn't move. "We're not done."

"Oh, yes, we are."

"It would be a lot easier if you told me where the money was, Grace."

"Do you always get paid for sex, Mr. Delamore?" she asked.

He studied her for a moment. "Don't play games with me, honey."

"Why not?" she asked. "You seem to enjoy them."

He shoved his plate away as if it had offended him. Apparently this morning wasn't going the way he wanted it to either. "I'm just telling you what I know."

"And I'm just asking you to leave. It was fun, Travis. But it certainly wasn't worth this."

He stood and slipped his wallet back into his pocket. "You'll hear from me again."

"This isn't high school," she said, following him to the door. "I won't be offended if you fail to call."

"No," he said as he stepped into the dry desert air. "You probably won't be offended. But you will be curious. This is just the beginning, Grace."

"One person's beginning is another person's ending," she said as she closed and locked the door behind him.

***

THE WORST THING she could do, she knew, was panic. So she made herself clean up the kitchen as if she didn't have a care in the world, and she left the curtains open so that he could see if he wanted to. Then she went to the shower, making it a long and hot. She tried to scrub all the traces of him off of her.

For the first time in her life, she felt cheap.

Embezzlement. Something had happened, something Michael was blaming on her. It would be easy enough, she supposed. She had disappeared. That looked suspicious enough. The new name, the new car, the new town, all of that added to the suspicion.

What had Michael done? And why?

She got out of the shower and toweled herself off. She was tempted to call Michael, but she certainly couldn't do it from the house. If she used her cell, the call would be traceable too. And if she went to a pay phone, she would attract even more suspicion. She had to consider that Travis Delamore was following her, spying on her.

In fact, she had to consider that he had been doing that for some time.

She went over all of their conversation, looking for clues, mistakes she might have made. She had told him very little, but he had asked a lot. Strangely—or perhaps not so strangely any more—all of their conversations had been about money.

Carole would have been proud of her. Grace had finally let her libido get the better of her. Alex would have been disgusted, reminding her that men couldn't be trusted.

What could he do to her besides cast suspicion? He was right. Without the money, he had nothing. And she had a job, no criminal record, and no suspicious investments.

But if he continued to follow her, she could go after him. The bartender had seen them leave her favorite bar together. She had an innocent face, she'd been living here for a year, got promoted, was well liked by her employer. Delamore had obviously flirted with her while he played poker the night before, and the casino had cameras.

They probably had records of all the times he had watched her before she noticed him.

It wouldn't take much to make a stalking charge. That would get her an injunction in the least, and it might scare him off.

Then she could find out why he was so sure he had something on her. Then she could find out what it was Michael had done.

***

THE NEWLY REMODELED ladies room on the third floor of the casino had twenty stalls and a lounge complete with smoking room. It had once been a small restroom, but the reconstruction had taken out the nearby men's room and replaced it with more stalls. The row of pay phones in the middle stayed, as a convenience to the customers.

Delamore wouldn't know that she called from those pay phones. No one would know.

She started using the third floor ladies room on her break and more than once had picked up the receiver on the third phone and dialed most of her old office number. She'd always stop before she hit the last digit, though. Her intuition told her that calling Michael would be wrong.

What if Delamore had a trace on Michael's line? What if the police did?

A week after her encounter with Delamore, a week in which she used the third floor ladies room more times than she could count, she suddenly realized what was wrong. Delamore didn't have anything on her except suspicion. He had clearly found her—that hadn't been hard, since she really hadn't been hiding from anyone—and he had probably checked her bank records for the money he assumed she had embezzled from her former clients. But the money she had gotten from the sale of the business was still in that hidden numbered account—and would stay there.

Her native caution had served her well once again.

She had nothing to hide. It didn't matter what some good-looking skip trace thought. Her life in Racine was in the past. A part of her past that she couldn't avoid, any more than she could avoid the scar on her breast—the scar that Delamore had clearly used to identify her, the bastard. But past was past, and until it hurt her present, she wasn't going to worry about it.

So she stopped making pilgrimages to the third floor women's room, and gradually, her worries over Delamore faded. She didn't see him for a week, and she assumed—wrongly—that it was all over.

***

HE SAT NEXT TO HER at the bar as if he had been doing it every day for years. He ordered a whiskey neat, and another "for the lady," just like men in her fantasies used to do. When he looked at her and smiled, she realized that the look didn't reach his eyes.

Maybe it never had.

"Miss me, darlin'?" he asked.

She picked up her purse, took out a five to cover her drink, and started to leave. He grabbed her wrist. His fingers were warm and dry, their touch no longer gentle. A shiver started in her back, but she willed the feeling away.

"Let go of me," she said.

"Now, Gracie, I think you should listen to what I have to say."

"Let go of me," she said in that same measured tone, "or I will scream so loud that everyone in the place will hear."

"Screams don't frighten me, doll."

"Maybe the police do. Believe me, *hon*, I will press charges."

His smile was slow and wide, but that flat look was in his eyes again, the one that told her he had all the cards. "I'm sure they'll be impressed," he said, reaching into his breast pocket with his free hand. "But I do believe a warrant trumps a tight grip on the arm."

He set a piece of paper down on the bar itself. The bartender, wiping away the remains of another customer's mess, glanced her way as if he were keeping an eye on her.

She didn't touch the paper, but she didn't shake Delamore's hand off her arm, either. She wasn't quite sure what to do.

He picked up the paper, shook it open, and she saw the strange bold-faced print of a legal document, her former name in the middle. "Tell you what, Gracie. How about we finish the talk we started the other morning in one of those dark, quiet booths over there?"

She was still staring at the paper, trying to comprehend it. It looked official enough. But then, she'd never seen a warrant for anyone's arrest before. She had only heard of them.

She had never imagined she'd see her own name on one.

She let Delamore lead her to a booth at the far end of the bar. He slid across the plastic, trying to pull her in beside him, but this time, she shook him off. She sat across from him, perched on the seat with her feet in the aisle, purse clutched on her lap. Flee position, Alex used to call it. You Might Be a Loser and I Reserve the Right to Find Someone Else, was Carole's name for it.

"If I bring you back to Wisconsin," he said, "I get a few thousand bucks. What it don't say on my card is that I'm a bounty hunter."

"What an exciting life you must lead," Grace said dryly.

He smiled. The look chilled her. She was beginning to wonder how she had ever found him attractive. "It's got its perks."

It was at that moment she decided she hated him. He would forever refer to her as a perk of the job, not as someone who had given herself to him freely, someone who had enjoyed the moment as much as he had.

All that gentleness in his fingers, all those murmured endearments. Lies.

She hated lies.

"But," he was saying, "I see a way to make a little more money here. I don't think you're a real threat to society. And you're a lot of fun, more fun than I would've expected, given how you lived before you moved here."

The bartender came over, his bar towel over his arm. "Want anything?"

He was speaking to her. He hadn't even looked at Delamore. The bartender was making sure she was all right.

"I don't know yet," she said. "Can you check back in five minutes?"

"Sure thing." This time he did look at Delamore, who grinned at him. The bartender shot him a warning glare.

"Wow," Delamore said as the bartender moved out of earshot. "You have a defender."

"You keep getting off track," Grace said.

Delamore shrugged. "I like talking to you."

"Well, I find talking with you rather dull."

He raised his eyebrows. "You didn't think so a few days ago."

"As I recall," she said, "we didn't do a lot talking."

His smile softened. "That's my memory too."

She clutched her purse tighter. It always looked so glamorous in the movies, finding the right person, having a night of great sex. And even if he rode off into the sunset never to be seen again, everything still had a glow of perfection to it.

Not the bits of sleaze, the hardness in his expression, the sense that what he wanted from her was something she couldn't give.

"You know, the papers said that Michael Holden went into your old office, and put a gun in his mouth and pulled the trigger. Then the police, after finding the body, discovered that most of the money your clients had entrusted to your firm had disappeared."

She couldn't suppress the small whimper of shock that rose in her throat.

Delamore noted it and his eyes brightened. "Now, you tell me what happened."

She had no idea. She had none at all. But she couldn't tell Delamore that. She didn't even know if the story was true.

It sounded true. But Delamore had lied before. For all she knew he was some kind of con man, out to get her because he smelled money.

He was watching her, his eyes glittering. She could barely control her expression. She needed to get away.

She stood, still clutching her purse like a schoolgirl.

"Planning to leave? I wouldn't do that if I were you." His voice had turned cold. A shiver ran down her spine, but she didn't move, just stared down at him unable to turn away.

"One call," he said softly, "and you'll get picked up by the Nevada police. You should sit down and hear what I have to say."

Her hands were shaking. She sat, feeling trapped. He had finally hooked her, even though she hadn't said a word.

He leaned forward. "Now listen to me, darling. I know you got the money. I been working this one a long time, and I dug up the records. Michael closed all those accounts right after you disappeared. That's not a coincidence."

Her mouth was dry. She wanted to swallow, but couldn't.

"'Member our talk about money? One of those first nights, here in this bar?"

She was staring at him, her eyes wide and dry as if she'd been driving and staring at the road for hours. It felt like she had forgotten to blink.

"I told you I don't need much, and that's true. But I'm getting tired of dragging people back to their parole officers or for their court date, or finding husbands who'd skipped out on their families and then getting paid five grand or two grand. Then people question your expenses, like you don't got a right to spend a night in a motel or eat three squares. Or they demand to know why you took so danged long to find someone who'd been hiding so good no cop could find them."

His voice was so soft she had to strain to hear it. In spite of herself, she leaned forward.

"I'm forty-five years old, doll," he said. "And I'm getting tired. You got one pretty little scar. Did you notice all the ones I got? On the job. Yours is the first case in a while where I didn't get a beating." Then he grinned. "At least, not a painful one."

She flushed, and her fingers tightened on the purse. Her hands were beginning to hurt. Part of her, a part she'd never heard from before, wanted to take that purse and club him in the face. But she didn't move. If she moved, she would lose any control she had.

"So," he said, "here's the deal. I like you. I didn't expect to, but I do. You're a pretty little thing, and smart as a whip, and this is probably going to be the only crime you'll ever commit, because you're one of those girls who just knows better, aren't you?"

She held her head rigidly, careful so that he wouldn't take the most subtle movement for a nod.

"And I think you got a damn fine deal here. The house is nice—lots of light—and the town obviously suits you. I met those friends of yours, the ball-buster and the one who thinks she's God's Gift to Men, and I gotta say it's clear why you left."

Her nails dug into the leather. Pain shot through the tender skin at the top of her fingers.

"I really don't wanna ruin your life. It's time I make a change in mine. You give me fifty grand, and I'll bury everything I found about you."

"Fifty thousand dollars?" Her voice was raspy with tension. "For the first payment?"

His eyes sparkled. "One-time deal."

She snorted. She knew better. Blackmailers never worked like that.

"And maybe I'll stick around. Get to know you a little better. I could fall in love with that house myself."

"Could you?" she asked, amazed at the dry tone she'd managed to maintain.

"Sure." He grinned. That had been the look that had made her go weak less than a week ago. Now it sent a chill through her. "You and me, we had something."

"Yeah," she said. "A one-night stand."

He laughed. "It could be more than that, darlin'. It took you long enough, but you might've just found Mr. Right."

"Seems to me you were the one who was searching." She stood. He didn't protest, and she was glad. She had to leave. If she stayed any longer, she'd say something she would regret.

She tucked her purse under her arm. "I assume the drink's on you," she said, and then she walked away.

He didn't follow her—at least not right away. And she drove in circles before going home, watching for his car behind hers, thinking about everything he had said. Thinking about her break, her freedom, the things she had done to create a new life.

The things that now made her look guilty of a crime she hadn't committed.

***

SHE DIDN'T SLEEP, of course. She couldn't. Her mind was too full—and her bed was no longer a private place. He'd been there, and some of him remained, a shadow, a laugh. After an hour of tossing and turning, she moved to the guest room and sat on the edge of the brand new unused mattress, clutching a blanket and thinking.

It was time to find out what had happened. Delamore knew who she was. She couldn't pretend any more. But he wasn't ready to turn her in. That gave her a little time.

She took a shower, made herself a pot of coffee, and a sandwich which she ate slowly. Then she went to her office, sat down in front of her computer and hesitated. The moment she logged on was the moment that all her movements could be traced. The moment she couldn't turn back from.

But she could testify to the conversation she'd had with Delamore, and the bartender would back her up. She wouldn't be able to hide her own identity should the police come for her, and so there was no reason to lie. She would simply say that she was concerned about her former business partner. She wanted to know if any of what Delamore told her was true.

It wouldn't seem like a confession to anyone but him.

She logged on, and used a search engine to find the news.

It didn't take her long. Amazing how many newspapers were online. Michael's death created quite a scandal in Racine, and the pictures of her office—the bloody mess still visible inside—were enough to make the ham on rye that she'd had a few moments ago turn in her stomach.

Michael. He'd been a good accountant. Thorough, exacting. Nervous. Always so nervous, afraid of making any kind of mistake.

Embezzlement? Why would he do that?

But that was what the papers had said. She dug farther, found the follow-up pieces. He'd raised cash, using clients' accounts, to bilk the company of a small fortune.

And Delamore was right. The dates matched up. Michael had stolen from her own clients to pay her for her own business. He had bought the business with stolen money.

She bowed her head, listening to the computer hum, counting her own breaths. She had never once questioned where he had gotten the money. She had figured he'd gotten a loan, had thought that maybe he'd finally learned the value of savings.

Michael. The man who took an advance on his paycheck once every six months. Michael, who had once told her he was too scared to invest on his own.

I wouldn't trust my own judgment, he had said.

Oh, the poor man. He had been right.

The trail did lead to her. The only reason Delamore couldn't point at her exactly was because she had stashed the cash in a blind account. And she hadn't touched it.

Not yet.

She'd been living entirely off her own savings, letting the money from the sale of her business draw interest. The nest egg for the future she hadn't planned yet.

Delamore wanted fifty thousand dollars from her. To give that to him, she'd have to tap the nest egg.

How many times would he make her tap it again? And again? Until it was gone, of course. Into his pocket. And then he'd turn her in.

She wiped her hand on her jeans. It was a nervous movement, meant to calm herself down. She had to think.

If the cops could trace her, they would have. They either didn't have enough on her or hadn't made the leap that Delamore had. And then she had confirmed his leap with the conversation tonight.

She got up and walked away from the computer. She wouldn't let him intrude. He had already taken over her bedroom. She needed to have a space here, in her office, without him.

There was no mention of her in the papers, nothing that suggested she was involved. The police would have contacted the Reno police if they had known where she was. Even if they had hired Delamore to track her, they might still not have been informed about her whereabouts. Delamore wanted money more than he wanted to inform the authorities about where she was.

Grace sat down in the chair near the window. The shade was drawn, but the spot was soothing nonetheless.

The police weren't her problem. Delamore was.

She already knew that he wouldn't be satisfied with one payment. She had to find a way to get rid of him.

She bowed her head. Even though she had done nothing criminal she was thinking like one. How did a woman get rid of a man she didn't want? She could get a court order, she supposed, forcing him to stay away from her. She could refuse to pay him and let the cards fall where they might. Years of legal hassle, maybe even an arrest. She would certainly lose her job. No casino would hire her, and she couldn't fall back on her CPA skills, not after being arrested for embezzlement.

Ignoring him wasn't an option either.

Then, there was the act of desperation. She could kill him. Somehow. She had always thought that murderers weren't methodical enough. Take an intelligent person, have her kill someone in a thoughtful way, and she would be able to get away with the crime.

Everywhere but in her own mind. No matter how hard she tried, no matter how much he threatened her, she couldn't kill Delamore.

There had to be another option. She had to do something. She just wasn't sure what it was.

She went back to the computer and looked at the last article she had downloaded. Michael had stolen from people she had known for years. People who had trusted her, believed in her and her word. People who had thought she had integrity.

She frowned. What must they think of her now? That she was an embezzler too? After all those years of work, did she want that behind her name?

Then again, why should she care about people she would never see again?

But she would see them every time she closed her eyes. Elderly Mrs. Vezzetti and her poodle, trusting Grace to handle her account because her husband, God rest his soul, had convinced her that numbers were too much for her pretty little head. Mr. Heitzkey who couldn't balance a checkbook if his life depended on it. Ms. Andersen, who had taken Grace's advice on ways to legally hide money from the IRS—and who had seemed so excited when it worked.

Grace sighed.

There was only one way to make this right. Only one way to clear her conscience and to clear Delamore out of her life.

She had to turn herself in.

***

SHE DID SOME MORE SURFING as she ate breakfast and found discount tickets to Chicago. She had to buy them round-trip from Chicago to Reno (God bless the casinos for their cheap airfare deals) and fly only the Reno to Chicago leg. Later she would buy another set, and not use part of it. Both of those tickets were cheaper than buying a single round-trip ticket out of Reno to Racine.

Grace made the reservation, hoping that Delamore wasn't tracking round trips that started somewhere else, and then she went to work. She claimed a family emergency, got a leave of absence, and hoped it would be enough.

She liked the world she built here. She didn't want to lose it because she hadn't been watching her back.

Twenty-four hours later, she and the car she rented in O'Hare were in Racine. The town hadn't changed. More churches than she saw out west, a few timid billboards for Native American Casinos, a factory outlet mall, and bars everywhere. The streets were grimy with the last of the sand laid down during the winter snow and ice. The trees were just beginning to bud, and the flowers were poking through the rich black dirt.

It felt as if she had gone back in time.

She wondered if she should call Alex and Carole, and then decided against it. What would she say to them, anyway? Instead, she checked into a hotel, unpacked, ate a mediocre room service meal, and slept as if she were dead.

Maybe in this city, she was.

***

THE DISTRICT ATTORNEY'S OFFICE was smaller than Grace's bathroom. There were four chairs, not enough for her, her lawyer, the three assistant district attorneys and the DA himself. She and her lawyer were allowed to sit, but the assistant DAs hovered around the bookshelves and desk like children who were waiting for their father to finish business. The DA himself sat behind a massive oak desk that dwarfed the tiny room.

Grace's lawyer, Maxine Jones, was from Milwaukee. Grace had done her research before she arrived and found the best defense attorney in Wisconsin. Grace knew that Maxine's services would cost her a lot—but Grace was gambling that she wouldn't need Maxine for more than a few days.

Maxine was a tall, robust woman who favored bright colors. In contrast she wore debutante jewelry—a simple gold chain, tiny diamond earrings—that accented her toffee-colored skin. The entire look made her seem both flamboyant and powerful, combinations that Grace was certain helped Maxine in court.

"My client," Maxine was saying, "came here on her own. You'll have to remember that, Mr. Lindstrom."

Harold Lindstrom, the district attorney, was in his fifties, with thinning gray hair and a runner's thinness. His gaze held no compassion as it fell on Grace.

"Only because a bounty hunter hired by the police department found her," Lindstrom said.

"Yes," Maxine said. "We'll concede that the bounty hunter was the one who informed her of the charges. But that's all. This man hounded her, harassed her, and tried to extort money out of her, money she did not have."

"Then she should have gone to the Reno police," Lindstrom said.

An assistant DA crossed her arms as if this discussion was making her uncomfortable. It was making

Grace uncomfortable. Never before had she been discussed as if she weren't there.

"It was easier to come here," Maxine said. "My client has a hunch, which if it's true, will negate the charges you have against her and against Michael Holden."

"Mr. Holden embezzled from his clients with the assistance of Ms. Reinhart."

"No. Mr. Holden followed standard procedure for the accounting firm."

"Embezzlement is standard procedure?" Lindstrom was looking directly at Grace.

Maxine put her manicured hand on Grace's knee, a reminder to remain quiet.

"No. But Mr. Holden, for reasons we don't know, decided to end his life, and since he now worked alone, no one knew where he was keeping the clients' funds. My client," Maxine added, as if she expected Grace to speak, "would like you to drop all charges against her and to charge Mr. Delamore with extortion. In exchange, she will testify against him, and she will also show you where the money is."

"Where she hid it, huh?" Lindstrom said. "No deal."

Maxine leaned forward. "You don't have a crime here. If you don't bargain with us, I'll go straight to the press, and you'll look like a fool. It seems to me that there's an election coming up."

Lindstrom's eyes narrowed. Grace held her breath. Maxine stared at him as if they were all playing a game of chicken. Maybe they were.

"Here's the deal," he said, "if her information checks out, then we'll drop the charges. We can't file against Delamore because the alleged crimes were committed in Nevada."

Maxine's hand left Grace's knee. Maxine templed her fingers and rested their painted tips against her chin. "Then, Harold, we'll simply have to file a suit against the city and the county for siccing him on my client. A multi-million dollar suit. We'll win, too. Because she came forward the moment she learned of a problem. She hasn't been in touch with anyone from here. Her family is dead, and her friends were never close. She had no way of knowing what was happening a thousand miles away until a man you people sent started harassing her."

"You said he's been harassing you for a month," Lindstrom said to Grace. "Why didn't you come forward before now?"

Grace looked at Maxine who nodded.

"Because," Grace said, "he didn't show me any proof of his claims until the night before I flew out. You can ask the bartender at the Silver Dollar. He saw the entire thing."

Lindstrom frowned at Maxine. "We want names and dates."

"You'll get them," Maxine said.

Lindstrom sighed. "All right. Let's hear it."

Grace's heart was pounding. Here was her moment. She suddenly found herself hoping they would all believe her. She had never lied with so much at stake before.

"Go ahead, Grace," Maxine said softly.

Grace nodded. "We had run into some trouble with our escrow service. Minor stuff, mostly rudeness on the part of the company. It was all irritating Michael. Many things were irritating him at that time, but we weren't close, so I didn't attribute it to anything except work."

The entire room had become quiet. She felt slightly lightheaded. She was forgetting to breathe. She forced herself to take a deep breath before continuing.

"In the week that I was leaving, Michael asked me how he could go about transferring everything from one escrow company to another. It required a lot of paperwork, and he didn't trust the company we were with. I thought he should have let them and the new company handle it, but he didn't want to."

She squeezed her hands together, reminded herself not to embellish too much. A simple lie was always best.

"We had accounts we had initially set up for clients in discreet banks. I told Michael to go to one of those banks, place the money in accounts there, and then when the new escrow accounts were established, to transfer the money to them. I warned him not to take longer than a day in the intermediate account."

"We have no record of such an account," the third district attorney said.

Grace nodded. "That's what I figured when I heard that he was being charged with embezzlement. I can give you the names of all the banks and the numbers of the accounts we were assigned. If the money's in one of them, then my name is clear."

"Depending on when the deposit was made," Lindstrom said. "And if the money's all there."

Grace's lightheadedness was growing. She hadn't realized how much effort bluffing took. But she did know she was covered on those details at least.

"You may go through my client's financial records," Maxine said. "All of her money is accounted for."

"Why wouldn't he have transferred the money to the new escrow accounts quickly, like you told him to?" Lindstrom asked.

"I don't know," Grace said.

"Depression is a confusing thing, Harold," Maxine said. "If he's like other people who've gotten very depressed, I'm sure things slipped. I'm sure this wasn't the only thing he failed to do. And you can bet I'd argue that in court."

"Why did you leave Racine so suddenly?" Lindstrom asked. "Your friends say you just vanished one night."

Grace let out a small breath. On this one she could be completely honest. "I had a scare. I thought I had breast cancer. The lumpectomy results came in the day I left. You can check with my doctor. I was planning to go after that—maybe a month or more—but I felt so free, that I just couldn't go back to my work. Something like that changes you, Mr. Lindstrom."

He grunted as if he didn't believe her. For the first time in the entire discussion, she felt herself get angry. She clenched her fingers so hard that her nails dug into her palms. She wouldn't say any more, just like Maxine had told her to.

"The banks?" Lindstrom asked.

Grace slipped a small leather-bound ledger toward him. She had spent a lot of time drawing that up by hand in different pens. She hoped it would be enough.

"The accounts are identified by numbers only. That's one of the reasons we liked the banks. If he started a new account, I won't know its number."

"If they're in the U.S., then we can get a court order to open them," Lindstrom said.

"Check these numbers first. Most of the accounts were inactive." She had to clutch her fingers together to keep them from trembling.

"All right," Lindstrom said and stood. Maxine and Grace stood as well. "If we discover that you're wrong—about anything—we'll arrest you, Ms. Reinhart. Do you understand?"

Grace nodded.

Maxine smiled. "We're sure you'll see it our way, Harold. But remember your promise. Get that creep away from Grace."

"Right now, your client's the one we're concerned with, Maxine." Lindstrom's cold gaze met Grace's. "I'm sure we'll be in touch."

***

GRACE THOUGHT the eight o'clock knock on her hotel room door was room service. She'd ordered another meal from them, unable to face old haunts and old friends. Until she had come back, she had never even been in a hotel in

Racine, so she felt as if she weren't anywhere near her old home. Now if she could only get the different local channels on the television set, her own delusion would be complete.

She undid the locks, opened the door, and stepped away so that the waiter could bring his cart/table inside.

Instead, Delamore pulled the door back. She was so surprised to see him that she didn't try to close him out. She scuttled away from him toward the nightstand, and fumbled behind her back for the phone.

His cheeks were red, and his eyes sparkling with fury. His anger was so palpable, she could feel it across the room.

"What kind of game are you playing?" he snapped, slamming the door closed.

She got the phone off the hook without turning around. "No game."

"It is a game. You got away from me, and then you come here, telling them that I've been threatening you."

"You have been threatening me." Her fingers found the bottom button on the phone—which she hoped was "0." If the hotel operator heard this, she'd have to call security.

"Of course I'd been threatening you! It's my job. You didn't want to come back here and I needed to drag you back. Any criminal would see that as a threat."

"Here's what you don't understand," Grace said as calmly as she could. "I'm not a criminal."

"Bullshit." Delamore took a step toward her. She backed up farther and the end table hit her thighs. Behind her she thought she heard a tinny voice ask a muted question. The operator, she hoped.

Grace held up a hand. "Come any closer and I'll scream."

"I haven't done anything to you. I've been trying to catch you."

She frowned. What was he talking about? And then she knew. The police had put a wire on him. The conversation was being taped. And they—he—was hoping that she'd incriminate herself.

"You're threatening me now," she said. "I haven't done anything. I talked to the DA today. I explained my situation and what I think Michael did. He's checking my story now."

"Your lies."

"No," Grace said. "You're the one who's lying, and I have no idea why."

"You bitch." He lowered his voice the angrier he got. Somehow she found that even more threatening.

"Stay away from me."

"Stop the act, Grace," he said. "It's just you and me. And we both know you're not afraid of anything."

Then the door burst open and two hotel security guards came in. Delamore turned and as he did, Grace said, "Oh, thank God. This man came into my room and he's threatening me."

The guards grabbed him. Delamore struggled, but the guards held him tightly. He glared at her. "You're lying again, Grace."

"No," she said and stepped away from the phone. He glanced down at the receiver, on its side on the table, and cursed. Even if he hadn't been wired, she had a witness.

The guards dragged him and Grace sank onto the bed, placing her head in her hands. She waited until the shaking stopped before she called Maxine.

***

GRACE HAD BEEN RIGHT. Delamore had been wearing a wire, and her ability to stay cool while he attacked had preserved her story. That incident, plus the fact that the DA's office had found the money exactly where she had said it would be, in the exact amount that they had been looking for, went a long way toward preserving her credibility. When detectives interviewed Michael's friends one final time, they all agreed he was agitated and depressed, but he would tell no one why. Without the embezzlement explanation, it simply sounded as if he were a miserable man driven to the brink by personal problems.

She had won, at least on that score. Her old clients would get their money back, and they would be off her conscience. And nothing, not even Delamore, would take their place.

Delamore was under arrest, charged with extortion, harassment, and attempting to tamper with a witness. Apparently, he'd faced similar complaints before, but they had never stuck. This time, it looked as if they would.

Grace would have to return to Racine to testify against him. But not for several months. And maybe, Maxine said, not even then. The hope was that Delamore would plea and save everyone the expense of a trial.

So, on her last night in Racine, perhaps forever, Grace got enough courage to call Alex and Carole. She didn't reach either of them; instead she had to leave a message on their voice mail, asking them to meet her at Oh Kaye's one final time.

Grace got there first. The place hadn't changed at all. There was still a jukebox in the corner and cocktail waitresses in short skirts and ankle boots with big heels. Tin stars and Wild West art on the walls, unstained wood and checkered tablecloths adding to the effect. High bar stools and a lot of lonely people.

Grace ignored them. She sashayed to the bar, slapped her hand on it, and ordered whiskey neat. A group of suits at a nearby table ogled her and she turned away.

She was there to diss men not to meet them.

Carole arrived first, black miniskirt, tight crop top, and cigarette in hand. She looked no different. She hugged Grace so hard that Grace thought her ribs would crack.

"Alex had me convinced you were dead."

Grace shook her head. "I was just sleeping around."

Carole grinned. "Fun, huh?"

Grace thought. The night had been fun. The aftermath hadn't been. But her life was certainly more exciting. She didn't know if the tradeoff was worth it.

Alex arrived a moment later. Her auburn hair had grown, and she was wearing boots beneath a long dress. The boots made her look even taller.

She didn't hug Grace.

"What the hell's the idea?" Alex snapped. "You vanished—kapoof! What kind of friend does that?"

In the past, Grace would have stammered something, then told Alex she was exactly right and Grace was wrong. This time, Grace set her whiskey down.

"I told you about my lumpectomy," Grace said. "You didn't care. I was scared. I told you that, and you didn't care. When I found out I didn't have cancer, I called you to celebrate, and you didn't care. Seems to me you vanished first."

Alex's cheeks were red. Carole stubbed her cigarette in an ashtray on the bar's wooden rail.

"Not fair," Alex said.

"That's what I thought," Grace said.

Carole looked from one to the other. Finally, she said, very softly, "I really missed you, Gracie."

"I thought some misogynistic asshole picked you up and killed you," Alex said.

"Could have happened," Grace said. "Maybe it nearly did."

"Here?" Carole asked. "At Oh Kaye's?"

Grace shook her head. "It's a long story. Are you both finally ready to listen to me?"

Carole tugged her miniskirt as if she could make it longer. "I want to hear it."

Alex picked up Grace's whiskey and tossed it back. Then she wiped off her mouth. "What did I tell you, Grace? Women always tolerate misogyny. You should have fought him off."

"I did," Grace said.

Alex's eyes widened. Carole laughed. "Our Gracie has grown up."

"No," Grace said. "I've always been grown-up. You're just noticing now."

"There's a story here," Alex said, slipping her arm through Grace's, "and I think I need to hear it."

"Me, too." Carole put her arm around Grace's shoulder. "Tell us about your adventures. I promise we'll listen."

Grace sighed. She'd love to tell them everything, but if she did, she'd screw up the case against Delamore. "Naw," Grace said. "Let's just have some drinks and talk about girl things."

"You gotta promise to tell us," Alex said.

"Okay," Grace said. "I promise. Now how about some whiskey?"

"Beer," Alex said.

"You see that cute guy over there?" Carole asked, pointing at the suits.

Grace grinned. Already, her adventure was forgotten. Nothing changed here at Oh Kaye's. Nothing except Cowboy Grace, who'd finally bellied up to the bar.

Jury Duty

PAMELA SAT in the center of the courtroom, not too close to the front because she didn't want to call attention to herself, and not in the back because she didn't want people to think she was hiding. She had done everything she could to blend in: she wore no make-up, and her clothes were Northwest business casual—a pair of brown slacks with an off-white sweater. With her left hand, she fingered her juror number—267—thoughtfully provided on a little wooden keychain so that she wouldn't lose it.

The court clerk pulled numbers out of a box and handed them to the judge. He was balding, and the top of his head shone in the fluorescent lights. His nasal voice boomed through the courtroom without the aid of a microphone, "Five-hundred-and-eighty-one. Five, eight, one."

As the unlucky man rose from his seat on the left side of the courtroom, the remaining members of the jury pool swiveled to watch him walk toward the jury box. Six people sat there already, hands folded, heads down, waiting.

The judge had said they would pick twenty-seven, enough for two juries and three extras. Both juries would listen to the case, although one jury would be designated as "alternate." The remaining three people were alternates also, added protection for a death penalty case that could last over a month.

Pamela had been called up two weeks ago, along with 1,000 others out of this county of 50,000, and she had stood in her kitchen, clutching the letter, feeling an uncomfortable sense of irony.

When she had come to Rickets Rock, a town so small that it seldom showed up on any map, she had decided that she would live as quietly as she could. She didn't want to draw attention to herself, good or bad. That meant getting a driver's license, registering to vote, being a good citizen. It meant concocting a history, and trying to smile at the locals. It meant lying, each and every day.

The jury summons had caught her in the lie: she couldn't back out because she had used a false name on her voter registration form. She had to go along with the fiction that she was Pamela Jackson, and hope that something about Pamela would keep her off the largest and most notorious jury the county had seen in decades.

"Juror thirty-four," the judge said. "Three-four."

A woman two seats from Pamela stood, and nearly tripped as she tried to get out of the row. Pamela kept turning her number over and over, the hard wood edges catching on her fingertips.

She had decided, when she had gone to orientation and received the outrageously long questionnaire, that she wouldn't lie if at all possible: she knew that trying to remember too many lies had tripped up more than one person.

So she had placed her personal views on the pages, thinking that they would disqualify her. Particularly the carefully worded questions on pages 10 through 13, the ones about law, the death penalty, and murder.

Question 33: Do you believe that some acts are so heinous that they can only be punished by death?

To which she had replied: *Yes.*

Question 50: Have you known or are you related to anyone who was murdered?

To which she had replied: *Yes.*

And *Question 117: Do you believe Raymond Northrup is guilty of the crimes of which he has been accused?*

To which she had replied: *I could care less.*

She had felt certain that the defense attorney, going through the questionnaires, would demand she be taken out of the jury pool, especially when she had had to explain her answer to question 50 on a later questionnaire. (*How was the deceased related to you?* Husband; *Explain the circumstances of the death:* He was a jackass. Of course, she didn't write that. Instead, she made up a lie about a beloved uncle who died in a convenience store robbery.)

"Two-sixty-seven," the judge said. "Two, six, seven."

Pamela's hand clenched around the number. She touched her round juror button, pinned to her sweater, and cursed silently. Her luck had abandoned her.

Now her goal was to be dismissed in the voir dire.

She grabbed her book—Patricia Cornwell's treatise on forensics and Jack the Ripper—and slung her purse over her shoulder.

Then Pamela eased out of the row, past the loggers and the truck drivers and the waitresses, and walked, head down, shoulders slumped forward, to the jury box.

Her heart was pounding. She had often pictured herself in a courtroom, but not here, not among the jury.

Instead, she expected to be at the tables, an attorney beside her, defending what was left of her miserable little life.

***

ANOTHER HALF HOUR went by before the rest of the twenty-seven victims were chosen. Then the questioning began, starting with the first juror picked, a dapper man who was the only person in the room, besides the attorneys, to wear a suit. Fifteen minutes into his voir dire, he was dismissed for claiming he did not have a strong stomach.

As he stepped down, the clerk drew a new number from the box, and another prospective juror took the first juror's place.

Pamela noted the excuse, and apparently so had the second juror. He made the same claim, which caused the judge to issue a gusty sigh.

"If we dismiss everyone with a weak stomach, we'll have no one left." He faced the defense attorney, who had posed the question. "If you believe these crimes are too graphic, we'll make sure there'll be no crime scene photos after lunch and we'll provide sickness bags, just like the airlines. Now, move on."

Pamela was the first up after the luncheon break. She returned to the courtroom loggy from the personal pan she'd had at the nearby Pizza Hut, and exhausted by a morning of listening to other people's lives.

During lunch she had toyed with changing her strategy, possibly saying that she did not approve of the death penalty or that she did not believe a person was innocent until proven guilty. But all of those answers would have contradicted her juror's questionnaire, a questionnaire that had informed her on the top of every page that her answers had the force of answers given under oath.

A new answer would call attention to her. If she was lucky, she would escape without much attention being paid to her at all.

Finally, the attorneys reached her. She had to repeat her name and her address.

"You own a bookstore, Ms. Jackson?" The prosecutor, Daphne Sullivan, stood in front of the jury box. She was a middle-aged woman who wore a stylish black suit that seemed out of place in this small county.

"Yes." Main Street Books, the new-and-used bookstore she had opened in what passed for Rickets Rock's downtown. When she had first received her jury letter, she had hoped that being a small business owner would disqualify her, but the clerk of courts had quizzed her, found out that she had a part-time assistant, and that the store sometimes closed when Pamela planned a day off, and decided that the store could afford to lose Pamela for a few weeks with little or no hardship.

"Do you enjoy reading?" Sullivan asked.

"Yes."

"Do you often read books like that one?" Sullivan nodded at the Cornwell.

"Yes." That was a deliberate lie, one concocted to get Pamela off the jury.

"Would you hold the book up so that everyone can see it?"

Pamela did. Her copy, a hardcover with a shiny dust, looked black and official.

"We won't have to worry about a weak stomach with this one," the judge muttered, even his soft words echoing throughout the courtroom.

"Do you watch *CSI*?" Sullivan asked.

"Sometimes," Pamela said.

"*Cold Case Files*? The forensics programs on The Learning Channel?"

"Sometimes," Pamela said.

"So you feel you have a grasp on the forensic side of police procedure?" Sullivan asked.

Pamela shrugged.

The judge said, "We'll need a verbal response for the record, Ms. Jackson."

"When you say 'a grasp,' I don't know what that means," Pamela said.

"Do you understand it?" Sullivan said.

"It's just science," Pamela said.

"And you understand science?"

Of course, you fool. I have more advanced degrees in biology and chemistry than you can dream up.

Pamela had to bite back the response. She wasn't a scientist now. She owned a bookstore. She was a mousy woman with mousy clothes who tried to disappear when people looked at her.

"I try to understand it," she said, which was as close to the truth as she could come.

"I have no problem with this juror," the prosecutor said, and turned toward the defense attorney, Jake Chivara.

He was too slick for this part of Oregon. His suit had the shine of silk, and his hands were manicured. His black hair had a layered cut that cost more than Pamela's entire outfit, but his eyes shone with an intelligence that she recognized as a match for her own.

He adjusted his suit coat as he walked toward the rail. "Do you consider murder your hobby?"

Her fingers clutched the book, its hard edges biting into her palm. "My *hobby*?"

He nodded toward the book she held. "You read about it. You watch television programs about it. You obviously think about it a lot."

True enough. She didn't like how perceptive he was. "I watch television programs about politics and biography and history, too, but I don't consider them my hobbies. I live alone. I run a bookstore. I read almost everything that comes through the door."

"But you brought that book for a reason, didn't you?" Chivara asked.

"To read while I waited," she said.

"You could have brought a romance novel," he said.

She shrugged. "I would have finished it in the time allowed. I wanted something that would last me all day."

"Be honest, Ms. Jackson. You brought that book so that we'd assume you know police procedure. You wanted to force us to kick you off the jury."

She looked at him in surprise and knew, at that moment, she had been caught. She had never been caught before, at least, not in her manipulations. It was a strange sensation.

Chivara smiled at her. "I don't like being manipulated, Ms. Jackson."

Pamela's hands slid on the book's cover. She was sweating.

"Your questionnaire says you believe that some crimes should be punished by death," Chivara said.

"Yes." She swallowed hard. This was the first time, in all of the questioning, that someone had mentioned the questionnaire.

"Does that mean you believe in the death penalty?" he asked.

"I haven't given it any thought." At least not in that way. The law was the law and she had nothing do with it. She didn't plan it nor could she change it. Human laws weren't immutable like scientific ones, but they existed and nowadays she did her best to live within them.

"Do you have a problem sending a man to his death?" he asked.

"Not in the right circumstances." Her answer had too much of an edge to it. She wished she could take the words back the moment she uttered them.

Chivara smiled again. "What sorts of circumstances, Ms. Jackson?"

Her mouth was dry. "I thought we were talking about the death penalty."

"We are. What circumstances? *These* circumstances?"

"If he did it," she said.

"Do you think he did it?" Chivara asked.

"I could care less," she said, repeating her answer from the questionnaire.

"Really? You don't care one way or another?"

She didn't like this attorney. He was irritating her. "Unless you put me on this jury, this crime has no impact on my life. I don't really care what that man did. I don't really care what the President does either, and he has a lot larger impact on my life than some petty murderer."

"Petty murderer," Chivara repeated softly. "You're quite interesting, Ms. Jackson. You know science and read about the law, but you say this case doesn't concern you. If we put you on the jury, would you care then?"

"Not really," she said. "I'd just be doing this because you're making me."

Chivara's smile became broad. "At least you're honest."

He walked back to his table, examined his notes, and then leaned over the railing, clearly speaking to his jury consultant.

Pamela's heart pounded hard. She tried to keep an impassive expression on her face, but she found it difficult. For the first time since she'd shown up in this courtroom, she was frightened.

After a moment, Chivara looked up.

"Ms. Jackson, do you know my client?" Chivara swept his arm toward the defendant. Until this moment, Pamela had refrained from looking at him.

She had seen his photograph on the county newspapers and once on the front page of the *Oregonian*, but she hadn't really looked at him. Nor had she looked at him the one or two times he waited on her.

"We've never formally met," she said.

"But you have met," the attorney said.

"He waited on me once at the Sneaker Wave," she said. "And at the Italian Noodle."

"Did you have a conversation?"

She shrugged, then added for the record, "Probably not."

"Probably not?" Chivara repeated.

"I go out alone with a book," she said. "I usually don't have conversations."

Truthful again.

Chivara's eyes narrowed, and she had the sense that he thought she was holding something back.

Chivara turned away, and she hoped he would dismiss her for cause. Instead, he said, "I have no problems with this juror."

The judge turned to her. "Is there any reason you believe you should not sit on this jury?"

Dozens. She had dozens of reasons, but none she could admit to. Neither attorney had given her a way out.

"I don't know if I can be impartial," she said, "given that I've met him."

The judge let out another of his gusty sighs. "The interactions you've had with the defendant are no different than sitting across a courtroom from him day in and day out. So give it a try, Ms. Jackson."

"Your honor," Chivara said, "this is why we wanted the trial moved."

"You made that motion and I dismissed it," the judge said. "If you want to try this case for the court of appeals and not for the jury, go ahead, Mr. Chivara. Otherwise, get over the loss and move on."

Pamela's cheeks were warm. Her ploy hadn't worked, might even have backfired.

"Juror two-six-seven," the judge said, "you'll be sitting on this case."

***

SINCE IT WAS the off-season, the cut-rate hotel that the court used to sequester juries was happy to have them. The jurors even got to have their own rooms, a luxury for which Pamela was grateful. She didn't like company in the best of circumstances, and this certainly was not the best of circumstances.

That first two days in the courtroom were difficult, especially for the other jurors. The prosecution laid out its case, and the defense gave its own theory of the crime. Most of the jurors were already familiar with the crime, but the details made them squeamish.

Pamela didn't mind the details, but she had trouble wrapping her mind around the crime at all.

Apparently, the defendant, Raymond Northrup, arrived home one afternoon in a rage. He shot his wife, his two daughters, and his infant son, supposedly planning to kill himself as well. In the end, he chickened out (or "came to his senses," as Prosecutor Sullivan said), and called 9-1-1 instead. The paramedics arrived to find a house filled with blood, and Ray Northrup sitting on the couch, watching reruns of *The Simpsons* as if nothing was wrong.

The prosecution promised pictures and the tape of the 9-1-1 call; the defense promised experts showing how the police botched the investigation, figuring that they already had the killer when, of course, the defense claimed, they had not.

Pamela listened with—she thought—clinical detachment, picturing both versions of the crime: a man pushed to his limits by bills, sick children and a nagging wife, hauling the shotgun out of the front closet and turning it on all of them; and the same man pushed to his limits, who arrived home after a hard day's work as a waiter (he could get nothing else in this small town) to find his entire family slaughtered.

But the clinical detachment didn't take, or perhaps it was a façade, designed to fool even herself. For that night, and two nights thereafter, Pamela had the nightmare, the one she had fled when she had come to Oregon.

The images were jumbled: Jason stumbling backwards, his hand up; Jason on the floor, his face gone; Jason's blood staining the wall beside their stove. She started to grab things—her ring, his watch, their checkbook, and then she set them down.

She knew better—even her dreamself knew better—and instead, she took the cash from the drawer, and the bike leaning against the old Billingsly house next door.

More images from before: the water from the shower draining pink; her clothing in the wash machine, the smell of bleach in the air; the half-eaten ham sandwich that had started it all.

She had been clutching it, trying to force it down, when he had walked in. *You can't do anything right*, she had said to him. *I wanted hot mustard, not sweet. Don't you ever listen?*

His voice, meek and soft, infuriated her, and at that moment, she woke up, covered in sweat, shaking, uncertain where she was, figuring at first it was some anonymous hotel on the trip west, then remembering how she had gotten herself into this new predicament years after the fact.

The hotel looked the same as the others: a double-bed barely bigger than the single she'd had in her first apartment; end-tables so cheap that if she leaned on them, they'd crack; a television set bolted to the dresser, and a double-size window with a single pane of glass so thin that it could shatter with the pressure of a determined fist.

Pamela got up and paced, her feet cold against the worn carpet. She was glad she was alone—who knew what she had cried out, what she had actually said?

That first night, she didn't go back to the bed, sleeping instead on the scratchy sofa, an equally scratchy blanket pulled over her scrunched-up form. She didn't sleep much and when she did, she dreamed of being uncomfortable, not of the past.

And she returned to that couch after every day of difficult testimony, after every photograph and replaying of the 9-1-1 call, until the clinical detachment she thought she had achieved that first day became an actual reality.

She could listen, store facts, theories, and opinions in one side of her brain, and kept them separate from the other side.

The emotion side.

The side that had always given her too much trouble.

***

THREE-PLUS WEEKS of testimony, arguments, breaks and confusion. Three-plus weeks of "retiring" to the jury room to wait while the lawyers and the judge worked something out. Three-plus weeks of small talk with people who probably never would have entered her store, people who probably hadn't voluntarily picked up a book in their lives, people who—with the exception of the transplanted Californian—had never lived anywhere but here.

Small minds with nothing but television and the trial to occupy them. Talk of the trial was off-limits until the testimony was over, so the Small Minds discussed the previous night's *Frasier* or the *Buffy* rerun or the late-night movie they were given on tape so they wouldn't watch the local news and talk shows.

She didn't watch any of it. She didn't discuss any of it either, preferring to read. The guards—at least they felt like guards—let her assistant deliver books, sometimes four and five a day, and Pamela read rather than socialized. So long as her mind was busy, her body remained calm.

The guards would paw through the bags, of course, verifying that everything Pamela's assistant brought were books, verifying that her assistant hadn't hid a newspaper article about the trial as a bookmark, verifying that there was no note advising her how to vote at the end of the trial.

But no one looked at the titles either. She finished the Cornwell, moved onto a history of the fingerprint, then followed that with a history of the corpse. A few tomes on forensics, a study of ballistics, and of course, dozens and dozens of novels—all shapes and sizes.

She read and thought and listened, and wished she had known all of this years ago, before she had come west. She would have done things oh so very differently. How easy it would have been to make it seem like *he* had gotten angry over the sandwich, *he* had hit her repeatedly, *he* had grabbed the gun.

But she hadn't known any of it. She had done the best she could with the little bits of knowledge she had, and she had managed to escape.

She lived here now, a new life she mostly enjoyed, and saw no use re-evaluating every second of the past.

***

THEN, FINALLY, the moment arrived. The closing arguments ended, the jury instructions were repeated *ad nauseum*, the defendant staring at jurors as if he were trying to fathom what each and every one of them were thinking.

This time, when they went into the jury room, there was a palpable sense of relief. The restrictions were off: they could discuss anything now, and the Small Minds all started to talk at once, offering opinions, offering advice, discussing what an ordeal they'd been through, how they couldn't stand the pictures.

Pamela couldn't stand the voices. Middle-class, grating, most of them with that slightly dulled speech she'd learned to recognize from locals. She sat in one of the upholstered chairs nearest the door, and wondered how she would get through this.

The jury room itself was small with two exits—one leading back into the courtroom, the other into the hallway. The room had no windows. Whoever had designed this room had certainly visited and obviously enjoyed the ambiance of hell's anteroom, because even the temperature was correct: hot enough to make the already small space seem unbearably stuffy.

"Right, Ms. Jackson?"

She heard her name and looked up. The transplanted Californian was looking at her. He was a wiry blond with a scraggly mustache whose rope-thin body and denim shirt made him look like a man who belonged outdoors, not trapped in a room furnished with modular office chairs and a cheap fake-wood conference table.

"I'm sorry," she said, peering at his name badge. Z. Wilson. She should have learned his name in the past few weeks. She should have learned all of their names, but of course, she hadn't.

"I said, I think we should get around to electing a foreman first, then talk about the case. What do you think?" His blue eyes studied her with an openness she didn't like. Obviously he expected her to be on his side.

"Looks like you're already doing a fine job," she said. "We don't need a vote."

"We'll vote." His voice had that irritated edge Jason used to get when she didn't give him the answer he liked.

She leaned back in her chair, deciding to give Z. Wilson some distance.

The woman who wore the giant silver cross on the front of her blouse each and every day reached to the center of the table and took twelve little pieces of paper from a notepad. Then she grabbed pencils and handed them out as if she were a school teacher.

She gave Pamela her paper and pencil last, smiling at her. Pamela did not smile back.

"Perhaps," said the Silver Cross, "perhaps we should say a small prayer so that God will guide our work."

"A small prayer?" Pamela asked, unable to keep silent in the face of this new irritation. "What kind of guidance do you want? Dearest God, please let us know if you want this killer to go free or if you want the state to fry him. Amen."

"Ms. Jackson," said the Californian. "That's enough."

She shrugged and pressed her lips together, but she had made her point. Two of the Small Minds who hadn't said anything yet—the first man chosen, and one of the other women—glared at Pamela as if she had killed the three children and the namby-pamby wife.

The wife, quite frankly, sounded like she deserved it, but the kids, well, Pamela didn't believe in killing kids. Kids couldn't be blamed for the situations they found themselves in. Only the parents were responsible for that.

"Write down the name of the person you think most suited for jury foreman," the Californian said. "Then put your paper in this little bowl next to the notepad. Don't sign your name."

"Why don't we just have a real election?" Pamela asked, clutching her pencil. "You and whoever else is enough of a control freak to want this idiot job?"

"You mean you?" another Small Mind asked.

"I don't want it," Pamela said.

"Vote for whomever you'd like," the Californian said.

Pamela sighed and shook her head. Then she wrote down *Z. Wilson: Because I believe in validating power grabs*, folded the paper into tiny squares and set it in the bowl.

Hers was the sixth. One Small Mind—a twenty-something man who was already going bald—chewed his pencil and looked from person to person before writing on his paper. He was the eleventh to put his vote in the bowl. The Silver Cross lady was the last, and she looked spooked.

"Mr. Acenan," the Californian said to yet another Small Mind, "would you mind reading the results? Mrs. Dunbar will tally them."

The Dunbar woman took another sheet of paper from the stack and held her pencil poised. The man dug inside the bowl, removed a piece of paper and read the results aloud.

Pamela wished she could take the book out of her purse. Who would've thought that average citizens would take this job so very seriously?

The Small Mind reading the papers had finally gotten to Pamela's. He glanced at her, his face flushed, and only read the name, not the commentary.

"You know," Pamela said mildly, "censorship is against the law."

"And you're a disgrace," the Small Mind said, still clutching her paper. "Can't you be serious about this?"

She thought of answering him honestly, but she knew the word "no" would piss him off. So she said, "I just want to get down to business. I've already lost a month of my life to this mess. I don't want to lose another one because you people dither."

"An election isn't dithering, Ms. Jackson," the Californian said.

"You've already taken over," Pamela said. "Why do we have to bother with the election?"

"Because," the Californian said, "it's part of the instructions. See? Item four. Elect a jury foreperson."

"You said foreman before. Can I change my vote?" Pamela asked. "I didn't consider any women."

Someone made a sound of disgust. Mrs. Dunbar said loudly, "We already have a majority for Mr. Wilson. So he is our fore*person*, unless there's an objection."

Pamela almost objected, just out of spite. She had to entertain herself somehow. But she was beginning to realize that her own antics might prolong this already painful situation, so she said nothing.

She crossed her arms and listened to Mr. California-Wilson read the jury instructions that the judge had already read to them, then ask if there were any questions that needed discussion or clarification before they got down to the "nitty-gritty."

Everyone said no, except Pamela, of course, who really didn't like the grade-school way this deliberation session was turning out. But she had decided to be quiet, and so she would be. She listened, or pretended to, while the jury discussed the rules, then reviewed the rules, and then discussed them even more.

Finally, at four o'clock, Mr. California-Wilson suggested that they take a preliminary vote—gosh! Just like the instructions suggested!—to see how far apart they all were. The vote would be anonymous, of course, and all the little pieces of paper would go into that damn bowl again.

She put her little piece of paper on top of her book, a novel called *A Certain Justice* which Pamela had chosen more out of irony than interest, and then paused.

She really hadn't given the fate of Mr. Raymond Northrup much thought, although she had done her part. She had listened, without prejudice and with that hard-won clinical detachment, to days and days of repetitive testimony, to argumentative lawyers and bad judicial rulings, to witnesses who hadn't known a damn thing and to witnesses who believed they had.

She had listened, she had absorbed, and she had come to no conclusion.

Yet they were asking her for one now. And if she was going to be the good citizen she was pretending to be, she had to give a real opinion. She supposed finding him guilty would get her out of here the quickest. After all, that was what the Small Minds seemed to believe, if their post-trial conversation was any indication.

But she couldn't write *guilty* on her piece of paper. Her hand froze over the page every single time. She was stunned to discover that the decision really did matter to her.

After all, she could have been the person sitting next to Chivara. She could have been pacing some jail cell right now, wondering if 12 disparate people would sentence her to a lifetime of imprisonment. She owed Northrup as much consideration as she had, mostly because she hoped someone would give her the same consideration if (when?) her time came.

She bit her lower lip, then glanced up at the bowl. It looked full. A number of the Small Minds were staring at her again.

Her hand shook over the paper. She gripped the pencil tightly and wrote *Not*, leaving off the guilty. She didn't want Mr. California-Wilson to misconstrue her intent.

She folded her piece of paper in half this time, just like everyone else had, and then she shoved it into the bowl. The Silver Cross woman grabbed it and handed it to California-Wilson as if he weren't capable of grabbing it himself.

He nodded toward the Dunbar woman and she got out yet another piece of paper so that she could tally the results.

Pamela expected more than one not-guilty vote. After all, it was pretty obvious that Northrup didn't have the balls to kill his entire family, no matter how angry and frustrated he got.

But she was the only not-guilty. California-Wilson tried not to ask for names, but she knew they'd find out, so she admitted it.

And that was when the clerk of the courts arrived, and told them to break for the night.

***

THE NEXT MORNING, the Small Minds had a game plan ready. They were going to review the evidence to convince her.

"Don't you want to know why I think he didn't do it?" Pamela asked.

"It doesn't matter what you think," Silver Cross said. "You obviously didn't care enough to listen."

"I listened," Pamela said. "I even made notes every evening. Did you people bother doing that?"

No one answered her. No one even looked at her.

"Look," she said. "I could change my vote so that we could get the hell out of here. Lord knows, I don't ever want to see you people again. But I don't think this guy did it, and I'm not going to send him to jail just because I want to sleep in my own bed tonight."

She was rather proud of herself. She sounded like a Real Citizen, like someone who cared about her fellow man.

"So," Mr. California-Wilson said with a notable lack of interest, "why do you think he didn't do it?"

"Because," Pamela said, careful to keep her tone respectful and polite, "he didn't run."

"Most people know better than to run," Wilson said.

"Most people know better than to kill their families," one of the Small Minds muttered.

"What?" Mrs. Dunbar asked.

The man shrugged. "I'm just saying if you're going to apply that kind of logic, then the whole case all falls apart."

The Small Minds argued among themselves for a long time, apparently forgetting that Pamela was the one they had to convince to change her mind. For a while, she thought she had convinced a few of them, but no.

They simply liked arguing.

And another day went by without any progress at all.

***

THE WEEK BLURRED into a series of questions and answers, followed by arguments.

"Ms. Jackson," someone asked at one point, "how can you think he didn't do it? He was covered in blood."

"So was the house," she said. "Didn't you look at the pictures? He sat on the couch, by his own admission. It was soaked in blood. Maybe he even hugged one of the kids like the defense attorney said. What would you do if you came home to your entire family dead?"

Of course, during the ensuing argument, she didn't say that she wouldn't have hugged a dead kid. But the arguments were never really about her, anyway.

"Ms. Jackson," one of the Small Minds said long about day three, "he told everybody at work that he was on edge, that he felt like he was going to explode. It's pretty clear that he did."

"Hell," she snapped. "I'm on edge. Does that mean I'm going to go on a rampage and kill you all to calm myself?"

It sounded tempting, but she knew better. She hadn't hurt anyone—deliberately—since she washed her husband's blood off her skin five years ago.

"Ms. Jackson," the Silver Cross idiot said to her on day five, "who else could have killed that family? Nothing was stolen and no one else even knew them, so no one else had a reason to kill them."

"You mean someone has a reason to kill an infant?" Pamela snapped. She ignored the wife. The wife bothered her. Pamela would have killed the wife given half a chance. Just because the woman hadn't been happy with her reproductive choices and her husband's inability to earn a living didn't give her the right to whine all the damn time.

Like these people were doing. The room really had to be bigger, much bigger, so that Pamela could pace.

She was alone and remained alone on this not-guilty thing. Even when she convinced the entire jury to go back into the courtroom and listen to the read-back of some testimony about the way that Northrup was found. His voice on the 9-1-1 tape, filled with emotion (she knew from personal experience that after killing someone, the emotion drained away), and the way he sat on that couch—as one cop put it—like he had nothing left to live for.

Ten days. Ten days they argued and fought and screamed at each other. (She didn't scream. She hated raised voices.) And they couldn't make her change her mind.

Ten days and 3 hours. The lunch break was when Mr. California-Wilson, whom she'd taken to calling the remaining Beach Boy to his face because he irritated her, knocked on the court-side door, and told the clerk that the jury was hung.

***

FASCINATING WORD, HUNG. Past tense of "hang," an active but unhappy word which meant to suspend or to die by hanging or to deadlock. All of those meanings had a little murder in them.

Just a little.

She had committed a killing after all.

And like the one she had committed before, she hadn't given it much thought until she actually completed the act. By then, the deed was done and she had to deal with it. It simply felt wrong to change her mind, as if she had lost a principle or something.

So when the judge polled the jurors—all of them, including her—and asked if there was any way to resolve the deadlock, she had spoken a forceful no.

The judge had no choice but to release the jury from its duty. The case was over, and the prosecutor had lost by one vote. The defense didn't cheer, although Northrup had looked for someone—anyone—to hug and got no volunteers.

Pamela filed back into the jury room with the Small Minds, happy she would never see them again, collected her things, and left the courthouse.

She had to go to the hotel to pack, and then she would be able to go home. Packing took longer than she expected—she had lived in this dive for nearly two months—and when it was over, she found that she would actually miss the place.

She'd learned to sleep in the bed, finally feeling like the ghost of Jason and his hideous death were behind her. The nightmare, completely gone.

It was almost as if she had been on trial and had forgiven herself.

The drive from the hotel to Rickets Rock took her past the courthouse. The cameras and crowds were gone. The place looked almost deserted. She was nearly past it when she realized that she had left her book inside.

She almost thought of donating it, then changed her mind.

She had donated enough to this stupid cause already.

She parked in the lot, just like she had on that very first day, and went inside by the front door. The anteroom was empty except for one of the court employees, sitting behind a counter.

The employee looked up, and clearly didn't recognize her. Pamela had taken off her juror button the moment they had been excused.

"May I help you?"

"I was on the Northrup jury," Pamela said, "and I left a book in the jury room."

The employee swiveled her chair, looked behind her, and reached down, lifting *A Certain Justice*. "This it?"

It was. Pamela had never summoned enough energy to read it. She thanked the woman, took the book, and turned.

"Ms. Jackson?"

The familiar voice sent a shiver through her. She looked over her shoulder. "Mr. Chivara. I thought you'd be off celebrating with your client."

Chivara smiled. It wasn't that predatory smile he used in court, but a rather wistful one. "I had a few things to get out of the courtroom. I see you did too."

She nodded, tucked the book under her arm, and started to leave. He kept pace with her.

"I understand you're the one who hung my jury," he said.

"So?" she asked.

"So," he said as he pushed open the door leading outside, "it surprised me."

"I'm sure it didn't, counselor," she said. "You picked me for some reason and it wasn't my good looks."

He laughed. The sound echoed across the empty street. "That's true. I thought you'd help my client, but not in this part of the case."

She stopped. "What does that mean?"

"It means, Ms. Jackson, we found that you lied on your jury questionnaire."

She felt cold. She knew better than to say anything. If she confirmed or denied, she would play right into his little game, whatever it was.

"And since we found that out, we figured we could use you as the basis for our appeal."

"You planned an appeal?" she asked.

"Every good defense attorney keeps one eye on the current case, and one eye on appeal. You were my ace-in-the-hole."

"I was your ace-in-the-hole when you picked me?"

"Now that wouldn't be quite right, now would it?" This time he gave her the predatory smile. "Of course, no one can prove when we learned that you didn't have a murdered uncle. Nor can they prove when we discovered that Pamela Jackson isn't your real name."

Her chill increased.

"Lying on a jury questionnaire is perjury, Ms. Jackson," Chivara said, "and I'm an officer of the court. Technically, I can't let you get away with that."

She forced herself to breathe. Then she turned around. "I can't say anything to you. You're accusing me and doing it in a do-you-beat-your-wife fashion."

"Am I?" he asked, his arms crossed.

"Besides," she said because she had to, because she couldn't keep silent, "if I did lie, and you discovered it, are you going to serve your client by reporting it? After all, I did hang your jury."

Chivara studied her for a long moment. "If I were still prosecuting, I'd already have you for identity fraud, and perjury. If I keep digging, what else would I find?"

A trail of temper, which had ceased. She had found her own kind of peace here in Seavy County.

"I like fiction, Mr. Chivara," she said. "We established that on the day of jury selection."

"You like crime dramas, Ms. Jackson," he said. "We never established that you liked only fiction."

She remembered the feeling she'd had that first day in the courtroom—that he was the only worthy adversary she had ever found. He was as smart as she was, which was a problem.

"We never established what lengths you'll go to in order to win a case," she said softly. "Looks like we'll learn that one today."

Then she turned around and headed down the steps to her car, feeling his gaze on her back. She half-expected to hear his footsteps following her, to feel his hand grab her arm, to pull her back and take her into that courtroom.

She'd be the one going to jail, and then she'd be the one going to trial, defended by someone like Chivara. Just like she'd imagined.

Just like she'd feared for the past five years.

But Chivara didn't follow her down the stairs. In fact, when she got into her car, and looked out the window, he was still watching her.

He had to choose between letting the client he had clearly thought guilty (after all, why else scheme for the appeal?) go free or letting a woman who had changed her identity and committed at least two small crimes that he knew of go free.

Poor Mr. Chivara. Such choices he had.

Such choices she had. Did she stay and pretend like nothing happened, trust the bastard to do what was in his best interest? Or did she run, again, losing all the money she'd put into her store and her home?

She clutched the key to her car. People who ran were guilty: she had argued that in the jury room, and her argument would come back to him. He'd know she'd done something.

But if she stayed, he'd have only his own conscious to wrestle with.

As a good defense attorney, he did that each and every day.

She put the key in the ignition and started the car. Chivara was still watching her.

She waved at him as she drove out of the parking lot.

Away from the courtroom and juries and the law.

Screw Chivara and his suspicions. She was going back to her store, her home and her life, her solitary life as a model citizen, a woman who did her duty and nothing more, just like everybody else.

Patriotic Gestures

Pamela Kinney heard the noise in her sleep—giggles, followed by the crunching of leaves. Later, she smelled smoke, faint and acrid, and realized that her neighbors were burning garbage in their fireplace again. She got up long enough to close the window and silently curse them; she hated it when they did illegal burning.

She forgot about it until the next morning. She stepped out her back door into the crisp fall morning, and found charred remains of her flag in the middle of her driveway. There'd been no wind during the night, fortunately, or all the evidence would have been gone.

Instead, there was a pile of burned fabric and a burn stain on the pavement. There were even footprints outlined in leaves.

She noted all of that with a professional's detachment—she'd eyeballed more than a thousand crime scenes—before the fabric itself caught her attention. Then the pain was sudden and swift, right above her heart, echoing through the breastbone and down her back.

Anyone else would have thought she was having a heart attack. But she wasn't, and she knew it. She'd had this feeling twice before, first when the officers came to her house and then when the chaplain handed her the folded flag which just a moment before had draped over her daughter's coffin.

Pamela had clung to that flag like she'd seen so many other military mothers do, and she suspected she had looked as lost as they had. Then, when she stood, that pain ran through her, dropping her back to the chair.

Her sons took her arms, and when she mentioned the pain, they dragged her to the emergency room. She had been late for her own daughter's wake, her chest sticky with adhesive from the cardiac machines and her hair smelling faintly of disinfectant.

And the feeling came back now, as she stared at the massacre before her. The flag, Jenny's flag, had been ripped from the front door and burned in her driveway.

Pamela made herself breathe. Then she rubbed that spot above her left breast, felt the pain spread throughout her body, burning her eyes and forming a lump in the back of her throat. But she held the tears back. She wouldn't give whoever had done this awful thing the satisfaction.

Finally she reached inside her purse for her cell, called Neil—she had trouble thinking of him as the sheriff after all the years she'd known him— and then she protected the scene until he arrived.

***

IT ONLY TOOK HIM five minutes. Halleysburg was still a small town, no matter how many Portlanders sprawled into the community, willing to make the one and a half hour one-way daily commute to the city's edge. Pamela had told the dispatch to make sure that Neil parked across the street so that any wind from his vehicle wouldn't move the leaves.

And she had asked for a second scene-of-the-crime kit because she didn't want to go inside and get hers. She didn't want to risk losing the crime scene with a moment of inattention.

Neil pulled onto the street. His car was an unwieldy Olds with a souped up engine and a reinforced frame. It could take a lot of punishment, and often did.

As a result, the paint covering the car's sides was fresh and clean, while the hood, roof and trunk looked like they were covered in dirt.

The sheriff was the same. Neil Karlyn was in his late fifties, balding, with a face that had seen too much sun. But his uniform was always new, always pristine, and never wrinkled. He'd been that way since college, a precise man with precise opinions about a difficult world.

He got out of the Olds and did not reach around back for a scene-of-the-crime kit. Annoyance threaded through her.

"Where's my kit?" she asked.

"Pam," he said gently, "it's a low-level property crime. It'll never go to trial and you know it."

"It's arson with malicious intent," she snapped. "That's a felony."

He sighed and studied her for a moment. He clearly recognized her tone. She'd used it often enough on him when they were students at the University of Oregon. When they were lovers on different sides of the political fence, and constantly on the verge of splitting up.

When they finally did, it had taken years for them to settle into a friendship. But settle they did. They hardly even fought any more.

He went back to the car, opened the back seat and removed the kit she'd requested. She crossed her arms, waiting as he walked toward her. He stopped at the edge of the curb, holding the kit tight against his leg.

"Even if you somehow get the D.A. to agree that this is a cockamamie felony, you know that processing the scene yourself taints the evidence."

"Why do you care so much?" she asked, hearing an edge in her voice that usually wasn't there. The challenge, unspoken: *It's my daughter's flag. It's like murdering her all over again.*

To his credit, Neil didn't try to soothe her with a platitude.

"It's the eighth flag this morning," he said. "It's not personal, Pam."

Her chin jutted out. "It is to me."

Neil looked down, his cheek moving. He was clenching his jaw, trying not to speak.

He didn't have to.

She understood the irony of the statement. Somewhere in her pile of college paraphernalia was a badly framed newspaper clipping that had once been the front page of the Portland *Oregonian*. She'd framed the clipping so that a photo dominated, a photo of a much-younger Pamela with long hair and a tie-dye t-shirt, front and center in a group of students, holding an American flag by a stick, watching as it burned.

God, she could still remember how that felt, to hold a flag up so that the wind caught it. How fabric had its own acrid odor, and how frightened she'd been at the desecration, even though she'd been the one to light the flag on fire.

She had been protesting the Vietnam War. It was that photo and the resulting brouhaha it caused, both on campus and in the State of Oregon itself, that had led to the final break-up with Neil.

He couldn't believe what she had done. Sometimes she couldn't either. But she felt her country was worth fighting for. So had he. He joined up not two months later.

To his credit, Neil didn't say anything about her own flag-burning as he handed her the kit. Instead he watched as she took photographs of the scene, scooped up the charred bits of fabric, and made a sketch of the footprint she found in the leaves.

She found another print in the yard, and that one she made a cast of. Then she dusted her front door for prints, trying not to cry as she did so.

"A flag is a flag is a flag," she used to say.

Until it draped over her daughter's coffin.

Until it became all she had left.

***

"I CALLED the local VFW, Mom," her son Stephen said over dinner that night. Stephen was her oldest and had been her support for thirty years, since the day his father walked out, never to return. "They're bringing another flag."

She stirred the mashed potatoes into the creamed corn on her plate. The meal had come from KFC: her sons had brought a bucket with her favorite sides, and told her not to argue with them about the fast food meal.

She wasn't arguing, but she didn't have much of an appetite.

They sat in the dining room, at the table that had once held four of them. Pamela had slid the fake rose centerpiece in front of Jenny's place, so she wouldn't have to think about her daughter.

It wasn't working.

"Another flag isn't the same, dumbass," Travis said. At thirty, he was the youngest, unmarried, still finding himself, a phrase she had come to hate.

The hell of it was, Travis was right. It wasn't the same. That flag these people had burned, that flag had comforted her. She had clung to it on the worst afternoon of her life, her fingers holding it tight, even at the emergency room, when the doctors wanted to pry it from her hands.

It had taken almost a week for her to let it go. Stephen had come over, Stephen and his pretty wife Elaine and their teenage daughters, Mandy and Liv. They'd brought KFC then, too, and talked about everything but the war.

Until it came time to take the flag away from Pamela.

Stephen had talked to her like she was a five-year-old who wanted to take her blankie to kindergarten. In the end, she'd handed the flag over. He'd been the one to find the old flagpole, the one she'd taken down when she bought the house, and he'd been the one to place the pole in the hanger outside the front door.

"The VFW says they replace flags all the time," Stephen said to his brother.

"Because some idiot burned one?" Travis asked.

Pamela's cheeks flushed.

"Because people lose them. Or moths eat them. Or sometimes, they get stolen," Stephen said.

"But not burned," Travis persisted.

Pamela swallowed. Travis didn't remember the newspaper photo, but Stephen probably did. It had hung over the console stereo she had gotten when her mother died, and it had been a teacher—Neil's first grade teacher? Pamela couldn't remember—who had seen it at a party and asked if she really wanted her children to see that before they could understand what it meant.

"I don't want another one," Pamela said.

"Mom…." Stephen started in his most reasonable voice.

She shook her head. "It's been a year. I need to move on."

"You don't move on from that kind of loss," Travis said, and she wondered how he knew. He didn't have children.

Then she looked at him, a large broad-shouldered man with tears in his eyes, and remembered that Jenny had been the one who walked him to school, who bathed him at night, who usually tucked him in. Jenny had done all that because Stephen at thirteen was already working to help his mom make ends meet, and Pamela was working two jobs herself, as well as attending community college to get her degree in forensic science and criminology. A pseudoscience degree, one of her almost-boyfriends had said. But it wasn't. She used science every day. She needed science like she needed air.

Like she needed to find out who had destroyed her daughter's flag.

"You don't move on," Pamela said.

Her boys watched her. Sometimes she could see the babies they had been in the lines of their mouths and the shape of their eyes. She still marveled at the way they had grown into men, large men who could carry her the way she used to carry them.

"But," she added, "you don't have to dwell on it, every moment of every day."

And yet she was dwelling. She couldn't stop. She never told her sons or anyone else, not even Neil who had become a closer friend in the year since Jenny had died. Neil, a widower now, a man who understood death the way that Pamela did. Neil, whose grandson had enlisted after 9/11 and had somehow made it back.

She was dwelling and there was only one way to stop. She had to use science to solve this. She couldn't think about it emotionally. She had to think about it clinically.

She had her evidence and she needed even more.

The next morning, the local paper ran an article on the burnings, and listed the addresses in the police log section. So Pamela visited the other crime scenes with her kit and her camera, identifying herself as an employee of the State Crime Lab.

Since *CSI* debuted on television, that identification opened doors for her. She didn't have to tell the other victims that she had been a victim too.

She took pictures of scorch marks on pavement and flag holders wrenched loose of their sockets. She removed flag bits from garbage cans, and studied footprints in the leaf-covered grass to see if they looked similar to the ones on her lawn.

And late that afternoon, as she stepped back to photograph yet another twisted flag holder beside a front door, she saw the glint of a camera hiding in a cobwebby corner of the door frame. The house was a starter, maybe 1200 square feet total. She wouldn't have expected a camera here.

"Do you have a security system?" she asked the homeowner, a woman Travis's age who looked like she hadn't slept in weeks. Her name was Becky something. Pamela hadn't really heard her last name in the introduction.

"My husband put it up," Becky said, her voice shaking a little. "I have no idea how it works."

"When will he be back?" Pamela asked.

Becky shrugged. "When they cancel stop-loss, I guess."

Pamela felt her breath slide out of her body. "He's in Iraq?"

Becky nodded. "I put the flag up for him, you know? And I haven't told him what happened to it. I've gotta find someone to fix the holder, and I have to get another flag."

Pamela looked at the house more closely. It needed paint. The bushes in front were overgrown. There were cobwebs all over the windows, and dry rot on the sills. Obviously the couple had purchased it expecting someone to work on it.

Either the money wasn't there, or the husband had planned to do the work himself.

"I can fix the holder," Pamela said. "If you have a few tools."

"My husband does," Becky said. "I can show them to you."

"I have a few things to finish, and then you can show me," Pamela said.

She dusted for prints, and then, for comparison, took Becky's and some off the husband's comb, which hadn't been touched since he left. Then Pamela went into his workroom, which also hadn't been touched, and took a hammer, some screws, and a screwdriver.

It took only ten minutes to repair the flag holder. But in that time, she'd made a friend.

"How'd you learn how to do that?" Becky asked.

"Raised three kids alone," Pamela said. "You realize there's not much you can't do, if you just try."

Becky nodded.

Pamela glanced at the camera. Untended since the husband left. It was probably in the same state of disrepair as the rest of the house.

"Can I see the security system?" she asked.

"It's not really a system," Becky said. "Just the cameras, and some motion sensors that're supposed to alert us when someone's on the property. But they clearly don't work any more."

"Let me see anyway," Pamela said.

Becky took her past the workroom, into a small closet filled with electronics. The closet was warm from the heat the panels gave off. Lights still blinked.

Pamela stared at it all, then touched the rewind button on the digital recorder. On the television monitor, she watched an image of herself fixing the flag holder.

"It looks like the camera's still working," she said. "Mind if I rewind farther?"

"Go ahead."

Backwards, she watched darkness turn to day. Saw Neil inspect the hanger. Saw Becky crying, then the tears evaporate into a stare of disbelief before she backed off the porch and away from the scene.

Back to the previous night. No porch light. Just images blurred in the darkness. Faces, not quite real, mostly turned away from the camera.

"Got a recordable DVD?" Pamela asked.

"Somewhere." Becky vanished into the house. Pamela studied the system, hoping that she wouldn't erase the information as she tried to record it.

She rewound again. Studied the faces, the half turned heads. She saw crew cuts and piercings and hoodies. Slouchy clothes worn by half the young people in Halleysburg.

Nothing to identify them. Nothing to separate them from everyone else in their age group.

Like her, her hair long, her jeans torn, as she stood front and center at the U of O, a burning flag before her.

She made herself study the machine, and figured out how to save the images to the disk's hard drive so that they wouldn't be erased. Then she inspected the buttons near the machine's DVD slot.

"Here," Becky said, thrusting a packet at her.

DVD-Rs, unopened, dust-covered. Pamela used a fingernail to break the seal, then pulled one out, and inserted it in the slot. She managed to record, but had no way to test. So she made a few more copies, feeling somewhat reassured that she could come back and try to download the images from the hard drive again.

"Will this catch them?" Becky asked while she watched the process.

"I don't know," Pamela said. "I hope so."

"It's just, they got so close, you know." Becky's voice shook. "I didn't know anyone could get that close."

It took Pamela a moment to understand what she meant. Becky meant that they had gotten close to the house. Close to her. The burning hadn't just upset her, it had frightened her, and made her feel vulnerable.

Odd. All it had done to Pamela was make her angry.

"Just lock up at night," Pamela said after a minute. "Locks deter ninety-percent of all thieves."

"And the remaining ten percent?"

They get in, Pamela almost said, but thought the better of it.

"They don't usually come to places like Halleysburg," she said. "Why would they? We all know each other here."

Becky nodded, seemingly reassured. Or maybe she just wanted to abandon an uncomfortable topic.

Pamela certainly did. She wanted to play with the images, see what she could find.

She wanted a solid image of the culprits, one that she could bring to Neil.

Maybe then, he would stop complaining that this was a petty property crime. Maybe then he might understand how important this really was.

***

BUT IT WAS her own words that replayed in her head later that night as she sat in front of her computer.

They don't usually come to places like Halleysburg.... We all know each other here.

She had lied to make Becky feel better, but the words hadn't felt like a lie. Thieves really didn't come here. There was no need. There was richer pickings in Portland or Salem or the nearby bedroom communities.

Besides, it was hard to commit a crime here without someone seeing you.

Except under cover of darkness.

Her home office was quiet. It overlooked the back yard, and she had never installed curtains on the window, preferring the view of the year-round flower garden she had planted. At the moment, her garden was full of browns and oranges, fall plants blooming despite the winter ahead. She had little lights beneath the plants, lights she usually kept off because they spiked her energy bill.

But she had them on now. She would probably have them on for some time to come.

Maybe Becky wasn't the only one who felt vulnerable.

Pamela put one of the DVDs in her computer, and opened the images. They played, much to her relief, so she copied the images to her hard drive and removed the DVD.

Her computer at home wasn't as good as her computer at work. But it would have to do.

She didn't want to do any work on this case at the State Crime Lab if she could help it. The lab was so understaffed and so overworked that it usually took four months to get something tested. When she last checked, more than 600 cases were backlogged, some of them dating back more than nine months.

Those cases were bigger than hers. The backlogs were semen samples from possible rapists and blood droplets from the scene of a multiple murder case.

She couldn't, in good conscience, bring something personal and private to the lab. She would work here as long as she could. Then if she couldn't finish here, she might be able to convince herself that the time she took at the lab would go toward an arson case—a serious one, not a petty property crime, as Neil had called it.

Petty property crime.

Funny that they would be on opposite sides of this issue too.

Pamela went through the images frame by frame, looking for clear faces. Her computer didn't have the face recognition software that one of the computers at the lab had, but she had installed a home version of image sharpening software. She used it to clean out the fuzz and to lighten the darkness, trying to find more than a chin or the corner of an ear.

Finally she got a small face just behind the flag, a serious white face with a frown—of disapproval? She couldn't tell—and a bit of an elongated chin. Enough to see the wisp of a beard—a boy's beard, more a wish of a beard than the real thing—and a tattooed hand coming up to catch the flag as the person almost blocking the camera yanked the pole out of the holder.

She blew up the image, softened it, fixed it, and then felt tears prick her eyes.

They don't usually come to places like Halleysburg.

No. They grew up here. And worked at the grocery store down the street to pay for their football uniforms at the underfunded high school. They collected coins in a can on Sunday afternoons for Boosters, and they smiled when they saw her and respectfully called her Mrs. Kinney and asked, with a little too much interest, how her granddaughters were doing.

"Jeremy Stallings," she whispered. "What the hell were you thinking?"

And she hoped she knew.

***

NEIL WOULDN'T let her sit in while he questioned Jeremy Stallings. He was appalled she'd even asked.

"That sort of thing belongs on TV and you know it," he'd said.

But she also knew he probably wouldn't do much more than slap the boy on the wrist, so what would be the harm? She hadn't made that argument, though.

Instead, she waited on the bench chair outside the sheriff's office conference room, which doubled as an interview room on days like this, and watched the parade of parents and lawyers as they trooped past.

No one acknowledged her. No one so much as looked at her. Not Reg Stallings, whose brother had sold her the house, or his wife June, who had taken over the PTA just before Travis got out of high school. No one mentioned the friendly exchanges at the high school football games or the hellos at the diner behind the movie theater. It was easier to forget all that and pretend they weren't neighbors than it was to acknowledge what was going on inside that room.

Then, finally, Jeremy came out. He was wearing his baggy pants with a Halo t-shirt hanging nearly to his knees. He wore that same frown he'd had as he took the flag off from Becky's front door.

He glanced at Pamela, then looked away, a blush working its way up the spider tattoo on his neck into his crew cut.

His parents and the lawyers led him away, as Neil reminded all of them to be in court the following morning.

Neil waited until they went through the front doors before coming over to Pamela.

She stood, her knees creaky from sitting so long. "He confess?"

Neil nodded. "And gave me the names of his buddies."

Pamela bit her lower lip. "Funny," she said, "he didn't strike me as the type to be a war protestor."

Neil rubbed his hands on his pristine shirt. "Is that what you thought?"

"Of course," Pamela said. "Every house he hit, we're all military families."

"Who happened to be flying flags, even at night." There was a bit of judgment in Neil's voice.

She knew what he was thinking. People who knew how to handle flags took them down at dusk. But she couldn't bear to touch hers. She hadn't asked Becky why hers remained up, but she would wager the reason was similar.

And it probably was for every other family Jeremy and his friends had targeted.

"That's the important factor?" she asked. "Night?"

"And beer," Neil said. "They lost a football game, went out and drank, and that fueled their anger. So they decided to act out."

"By burning flags?" Her voice rose.

"A few weeks before, they knocked down mailboxes. I'm going to hate to charge them. There won't be much left of the football team."

"That's all right," Pamela said bitterly. "Petty property crimes shouldn't take them off the roster long."

"It's going to be more than that," Neil said. "They're showing a destructive pattern. This one isn't going to be fun."

"For any of us," Pamela said.

***

HER HANDS were shaking as she left. She had wanted the crime to mean something. The flag had meant something to her. It should have meant something to them too.

God, Mom, for an old hippie, you're such a prude. Jenny's voice, so close that Pamela actually looked around, expecting to see her daughter's face.

"I'm not a prude," she whispered, and then realized she was reliving an old argument between them.

Sure you are. Judgmental and dried up. I thought you protested so that people could do what they wanted.

Pamela sat in the car, her creaky knees no longer holding her.

No, I protested so that people wouldn't have to die in another senseless war, she had said to her daughter on that May afternoon.

What year was that?

It had to be 1990, just before Jenny graduated from high school.

I'm not going to die in a stupid war, Jenny had said with such conviction that Pamela almost believed her. *We don't do wars any more. I'm going to get an education. That way, you don't have to struggle to pay for Travis. I know how hard it's been with Steve.*

Jenny, taking care of things. Jenny, who wasn't going to let her cash-strapped mother pay for her education. Jenny, being so sure of herself, so sure that the peace she'd known most of her life would continue.

To Jenny, going into the military to get a free education hadn't been a gamble at all.

Things'll change, honey, Pamela had said. *They always do.*

And by then I'll be out. I'll be educated, and moving on with my life.

Only Jenny hadn't moved on. She'd liked the military. After the First Gulf War, she'd gone to officer training, one of the first women to do it.

I'm a feminist, Mom, just like you, she'd said when she told Pamela.

Pamela had smiled, keeping her response to herself. She hadn't been that kind of feminist. She wouldn't have stayed in the military. She wasn't sure she believed in the military—not then.

And now? She wasn't sure what she believed. All she knew was that she had become a military mother, one who cried when a flag was burned.

Not just a flag.

Jenny's flag.

And that's when Pamela knew.

She wanted the crime to mean something, so she would make sure that it did.

***

SHE BROUGHT her memories to court. Not just the scrapbooks she'd kept for Jenny, like she had for all three kids, but the pictures from her own past, including the badly framed front page of the *Oregonian*.

Five burly boys had destroyed Jenny's flag. They stood in a row, their lawyers beside them, and pled to misdemeanors. Their parents sat on the blond bench seats in the 1970s courtroom. A reporter from the local paper took notes in the back. The judge listened to the pleadings.

Otherwise, the room was empty. No one cheered when the judge gave the boys six months of counseling. No one complained at the nine months of community service and even though a few of them winced when the judge announced the huge fines that they (and not their parents) had to pay, no one said a word.

Until Pamela asked if she could speak.

The judge—primed by Neil—let her.

Only she really didn't speak. She showed them Jenny. From the baby pictures to the dress uniform. From the brave eleven-year-old walking her brother to school to the dust-covered woman who had smiled with some Iraqi children in Baghdad.

Then Pamela showed them her *Oregonian* cover.

"I thought you were protesting," she said to the boys. "I thought you trying to let someone know that you don't approve of what your country is doing."

Her voice was shaking.

"I thought you were being patriotic." She shook her head. "And instead you were just being stupid."

To their credit, they watched her. They listened. She couldn't tell if they understood. If they knew how her heart ached—not that sharp pain she'd felt when she found the flag, but just an ache for everything she'd lost.

Including the idealism of the girl in the picture. And the idealism of the girl she'd raised.

When she finished, she sat down. And she didn't move as the judge gaveled the session closed. She didn't look up as some of the boys tried to apologize. And she didn't watch as their parents hustled them out of court.

Finally, Neil sat beside her. He picked up the framed *Oregonian* photograph in his big, scarred hands.

"Do you regret it?" he asked.

She touched the edge of the frame.

"No," she said.

"Because it was a protest?"

She shook her head. She couldn't articulate it. The anger, the rage, the fear she had felt then. Which had been nothing like the fear she had felt every day her daughter had been overseas.

The fear she felt now when she looked at Stephen's daughters and wondered what they'd choose in this never-ending war.

"If I hadn't burned that flag," she said, "I wouldn't have had Jenny."

Because she might have married Neil. And even if they had made babies, none of those babies would have been Jenny or Stephen or Travis. There would have been other babies who would have grown into other people.

Neil wasn't insulted. They had known each other too long for insults. Instead, he put his hand over hers. It felt warm and good and familiar. She put her head on his shoulder.

And they sat like that, until the court reconvened an hour later, for another crime, another upset family, and another broken heart.

Spinning

MIDWAY THROUGH that first awful class—when the clock above the mirrors said she had only been on the stationary bike for 22 minutes, but her body told her she had been on it for 2.2 days, when she thought her heart was going to burst through her chest like a creature out of the movie *Alien*, when sweat poured off her in rivers, and her breath came in deep honking gasps—midway through all of that, Patricia bent her head, saw the flab on her thighs go up while her actual legs went down, and heard Tom, her instructor, call over the rock music:

"Good. Real good. Excellent. Keep going. Wonderful. Hmmm. You'll get it. Relax. Wait until it feels good. Good. Relax...."

Something in the rhythm of his voice, in the involuntary nature of the sounds, told her he would sound like this in bed. He would talk, his words meaningless, an accompaniment to the beat his body had established, and the pattern would continue building, building, building, until his voice rose in a cry and everything stopped.

She focused on that, held onto that, because it felt like the only thing that made him real somehow, made him, this Greek god of a man, whose muscles were perfectly sculpted, whose eyes were warm and brown and not-quite-sympathetic-enough, slightly less intimidating. And she needed a reason not to be intimidated.

Two hundred pounds did not fit on her delicate five-four frame. She didn't know how she had let herself go like this. Excuse after excuse, she supposed, a sense of denial, a willingness to believe, at first, that it was her clothes that were shrinking, not her body that was expanding. It had taken two years of failed exercise attempts that had brought her to this class, to this moment, and she had been planning to drop out of this one until he fell into his unconscious personal rhythm, until she realized that he too was human.

And then she looked up, saw those not-quite-sympathetic eyes fall on her with something like disgust. She knew how she looked. The gym had thoughtfully provided a mirror in its exercise room. She saw the five other women in the spinning class: the darling with her tight sculpted 25-year-old body who made it clear that she had never tried this before, and who was so in shape that she managed all the motions with ease; the middle-aged housewives in the middle, looking fine to her, but complaining about that extra ten pounds they always put on in the holidays; the bartender, an older woman who looked strong and solid, who had told Patricia about the class; and the anorexic creature beside Patricia who was having just as much trouble keeping up—apparently her eating habits, like Patricia's, robbed her of the strength to exercise. But none of them looked as disgusting as she did in her sweats, her face red, her new perm damp, her body straining. Why was it that she, a woman who had to struggle to walk across the room, was being treated like the pariah, when she was the one who needed the most courage, the most strength, to be here?

It was because the others were all afraid that some day, somehow, through the same careless inattentiveness that she had shown, they would all end up looking like her.

But *he*, he had no right to look at her that way. He was supposed to be the professional, the one who helped people like her become hard bodies like him. He wasn't supposed to let her see that she disgusted him, even though she did.

It was that look, in combination with her realization about him, that gave her the determination she had lacked. As her legs went round and round, the stationary bike's resistance on its lowest setting, she realized that she now had a goal.

She had been pretty once, eighty pounds and fifteen years ago. She would be pretty again.

And when she was, he would want her. She would take him to bed, and she would find out if he really sounded like that. And if he did, she would look at him with the same disgust she had seen in his eyes only moments before. She would look at him, and she would laugh.

***

Meeting her goal was harder than she thought it would be. After her first spinning class, she had to go immediately to bed and when she got up the next morning, her legs ached so badly that she could barely climb stairs. Over time, she grew used to the class, and she moved onto weights, treadmills, and aerobics.

Within six months, she had lost thirty pounds and her body had definition. The spinning classes were tedious—she had learned the pattern within a few days and knew what he would call out next—and she found herself waiting for a repetition of the moment, the moment that had inspired her. It didn't happen often, and she watched him now. He would catch himself, as if he did know how he sounded, and sometimes, he would catch her looking at him.

She always smiled. She tried to be as congenial as she could.

Fortunately, she didn't have to be congenial anywhere else. She was having trouble being pleasant. The exercise put her in a good mood for an hour or two afterward, but the exhaustion that came with it angered her. She went back to her family doctor, wondering if the exercise was hurting her (even though he claimed, up front, that it would be the best thing for her) and he had calmly, patiently, explained how the human body worked.

She got a sense that he gave this explanation a lot. *You are carrying the weight of a 12-year-old girl in addition to your own body weight. It is as if you are doing these exercises for two, when everyone else in the room was doing them for one.*

She wished she could explain it to them. The looks had stopped, after her second month, except when newcomers entered the gym. Then they stared at her as if she were the freak, or the one that would fail, and eventually, they would disappear.

She remained, tenacious to the last.

***

IT WAS AT HER JOB, another twenty pounds later, that she realized she was in a revenge cycle. She worked as a website designer for a local internet provider. Her brother was her boss, and he would interview the customer on tape, and she would listen to the interview, use the materials, and design the website from there.

In the past two weeks, clients who came to the office (and there were so few of them: most of them as lonely as she was) began to compliment her on her looks. She did look better. The loss of fifty pounds had also taken ten years off her face. The exercise and all the water it forced her to drink had cleared up her skin, and the pretty girl she remembered was beginning to make appearances in her mirror.

The office was a tiny place—a three-room suite with a door opening onto a strip mall sidewalk—that became even tinier whenever someone new came inside. The wallpaper-thin walls did not shut out any sound, so she usually heard her brother's interviews with potential website clients twice. Those she didn't mind, because she made notes, hearing different things on the first and second listenings. It was the casual conversations, the folks who dropped in just to update their accounts or to gossip with her brother or to see, lately, how different Patricia was looking, that got on her nerves.

She had taken to closing her presswood door and opening the window that overlooked the alley, no matter how cold it was. Sometimes, if she did that, she could focus on the whoosh of traffic on the highway, the crunch of wheels on the gravel, the occasional conversations of people entering other businesses. If she was really lucky, it all became white noise, a sort of background to the tap-tap-tap of her fingers on the keys, her mind not in Seavy Village, but inside the computer, in that vast and somewhat mysterious network of computers known as the internet. There she could float, be someone else, anyone else, and no one seemed to care that she was different except her.

It was in one of those moments when, on a whim, she took the quiz the local psychiatrist had asked her to put on his website. His self-help book, *Negative Thoughts and How to Cure Them*, had been climbing the bestseller list, and he believed he needed a way for his fans to contact him. He thought the quiz was an open door. She hadn't been too sure, but then, she hadn't been too sure about his book either, which seemed to her (when she read it) a '90s rip-off of Napoleon Hill's classic *Think and Grow Rich*. But she, like the suckers she was designing the page for, took the quiz and as she read the paragraph summary of her answers, she saw herself in its analysis:

You have a tendency to blame others for your problems. Instead of solving those problems, you hope that others suffer worse than you have. Sometimes you fantasize about causing the suffering yourself. This is not healthy behavior. For a solution, see page 62 in my book...

And because she had already committed herself that far, she looked up page 62 in the complementary copy of the book that the psychiatrist had given the office, and saw the chapter heading in bold: *The Revenge Cycle: Explanations of Your Obsession and How to Cure it.*

Surprisingly, the advice made sense to her. She had focused—obsessed—on Tom, on the sound of his voice, on the revenge she would get once she had sex with him and more importantly, had laughed at him. Had humiliated him with her voice and her eyes, and the body she had sculpted for just that purpose.

After reading the chapter, she stood up behind her desk, ran her hands down her arms, feeling the skin beneath her cotton blouse. The skin and the muscle and the bone. She hadn't felt bone in years, the sharpness of her elbows, the two bumps on either side of her wrists. She was beginning to like this new self, beginning to accept that it, and not the woman whose thighs brushed together, was who she was.

If she ended her focus on Tom, perhaps the exercise would end too. After all, the book said that all behaviors relating to the revenge cycle had to stop in order for it to be cured.

The only behaviors she had were the good ones; the exercise, the healthy food; the grooming that she had only recently started to do again. Clothes looked good once more. Makeup made her seem older and more mysterious rather than a woman denying her encroaching middle age.

As revenge fantasies went, this was a fairly harmless one. Perhaps she might dent Tom's rather solid self-esteem. Perhaps she might even make him reconsider casual affairs. But those two things might be good for him.

They would certainly be good for her.

It felt, when she looked on that moment later, as if for one brief afternoon, she surfaced from her own thoughts, had a sense of clarity, and then dove back in, like a whale coming to the surface of water to take a breath.

She didn't take another breath for a very long time.

***

AT THE END of eighteen months, she thought of spinning class as hell. But she hit her ideal weight that month, and actually came to the class in spandex that made her look athletic and not like she had squeezed her bulk into someone else's clothes. As she went through her first class at her perfect weight, she listened for the moment when Tom's voice rose, when it punctuated each word with a gasping sexual rhythm, and when it did, she looked at him and found him looking at her.

The not-quite-sympathetic expression had left his eyes a long time ago, replaced by a kind of pride. She actually overheard him talking to the aerobics instructor, using Patricia as an example of how well spinning worked. She studied him as her legs worked—thighs like steel now, muscles rippling beneath hard skin—and then, slowly, she smiled.

She had been saving her smiles. They had been her best feature even when she was heavy, and she had rationed them, at least for him. She wanted to use them when she was in peak condition, knowing that he would be attracted not so much to her face as to her sculpted form. And so, as their eyes met and the smile creased her face, she saw something new. She saw his eyebrows rise briefly and knew that small movement for something she hadn't seen in years.

Flirting.

She raised her eyebrows in return, and then looked away. First salvo sent and received. Mating dance initiated. Humiliation about to begin.

She went home that night happy for the first time since she had started taking spinning classes. In her two room apartment whose ocean view was the only thing to recommend it, she danced a small jig, and then smiled again.

Her plan would actually work.

***

SHE DIDN'T KNOW what would happen after she slept with him. That was the problem she was working on as she drove to the gym in her beloved 1974 Volkswagen Bug. It smelled of oil and it vibrated crazily, but she had owned that car since she bought it used in high school and it had been the one thing she had maintained through all the years.

Her job at the IP had begun to pay her real money and she could buy a good car for the first time in her life, but she didn't. She couldn't give up her faithful Bug. She never would. She did her best thinking in it. And as she drove up the hill to the gym, she needed a goal that would last her past her revenge on Tom. And, if she were going to be truly healthy, it had to be one that did not continue to play out her revenge fantasy.

She parked in her usual space, grabbed her gym bag, and got out, startled to see a police car parked beside the bicycle racks. In the two years she had been coming here, she had never seen a police car. But there was that one month when a paramedic tried to fit exercise into his schedule. Sometimes he parked an ambulance outside. That had unnerved her the first time as well.

She pushed her car door shut with her hip, walked around the police car, and headed down the flight of stairs to the club itself. There she saw two policemen at the front desk and the aerobics instructor, a petite thing with too much energy for a human being, sitting on a stool looking stricken. No one was on the machines, and even the hardcore gym rats who spent hours on the free weights, were huddled near the Nautilus equipment. From there, any conversation at the front desk could be heard, loud and clear.

Patricia opened the glass door and came inside. She walked to the desk like she always did, to sign in and pay the extra fee for her special class, when a look from one of the policeman stopped her. The aerobics instructor, whose name she had never learned, raised liquid brown eyes filled with tears.

"There's no class," she said in a shaky voice. "Tom is dead."

The words circled in her head like the wheels on the stationary bike. *Tom. Is. Dead.* He couldn't be dead. She wasn't finished yet. She hadn't had the answer to her question, she hadn't been able to look at him with not-quite-sympathy in her eyes.

The police were watching her reaction. And she looked at them, truly seeing them for the first time. The man closest to her was about her age, fifty pounds overweight and carrying it all in the danger zone around his stomach. The other man was younger, athletic, broad-shouldered. His blue eyes were sharp, his lips thin. He didn't seem to miss anything. Especially the expression that must have crossed her face. What had it looked like? Shock? Disappointment?

Fear?

For her first response, after that flash of what-about-me? was guilt. She could have done it. She *had* done it, a thousand times, in her mind. Not killed him physically, but emotionally. Somehow she thought her contempt would destroy him.

Arrogant, of course, but arrogance was what got her through.

The younger officer stepped forward. "Did you know Tom Ansara?"

Not well enough to know his last name. Maybe not at all. "I saw him three times a week," she said. "But I didn't know him. He instructed my spinning class."

But she had a hunch about how he sounded in bed. It felt as if she had been intimate with him. It felt as if she had lost someone close.

She wanted to put her hand on the wall, on the chair, to use something for support.

Those sharp blue cop eyes watched her, seeing everything. How good an actress was she? She didn't know. Good, she hoped. Good enough.

"And you are?"

"Patricia," she said, giving her first name only as she always did at the gym. Only after a moment, she added, "Taylor. Patricia Taylor."

With that little pause in there, her last name sounded made up, even to her. She fumbled with her purse. "I have i.d."

"No need," the cop said. "Just wait with the others."

She carried her gym bag and her coat to the nearest table, littered with out-of-date health and fitness magazines. In her 18 months at the gym, she had never sat here. She had never spent any time sitting on anything that didn't spin or move or have weights attached.

The gym seemed excessively silent. The usual loud rock and roll music had been turned off. Someone had muted all three television sets. A fan whirred in the corner, set to cool whomever had been on the Precor cross-training machine, but that person had been off the machine for so long that the digitized program was running on the computer screen. In the long mirror lining one wall, she could see the racquetball bleachers. The Thursday night wallyball players were seated there, heads bowed, hands threaded and hanging over their knees.

No one spoke. It was as if the cops were playing Agatha Christie, waiting until all the suspects arrived before going through the list and coming up with the killer.

The other members of the spinning class threaded in: the darling, the middle-aged housewives, and the bartender. One by one they all took seats at the table, as if united in the class that no longer existed. The anorexic had given up long ago, and had been replaced by the only man, an accountant with a hairy back and a tendency to take off his shirt at precisely 33 minutes into the session. In street clothes, he looked diminished and not at all like a man who wore a white muscle T and baggy gym shorts cut one size too small.

The aerobics instructor sobbed her line each time a class member entered as if she were a model trying out for a play. The shock seemed similar for all of them. Only the darling asked if it was all right if she exercised while she waited. The incredulous silence that greeted her question was her answer, and even she realized that she had said something wrong.

The clock above the mirror showed that forty-five minutes had passed since Patricia arrived. On a normal night, she would be sweating through the last fifteen minutes of the routine, wondering if he would forget himself again and provide her with enough ammunition to survive another week. Instead, she was sitting as still as she possibly could in a white plastic chair, wondering if the police meant to hold them all night.

Clearly Tom's death was suspicious, and clearly it involved people from the gym. Unless he had no other life but the gym. It surprised her to realize that she knew nothing about him, not really. She hadn't even figured out which car in the driveway was his. She had been able to tell, from the way he spoke in class, that he rode his bicycle a lot outdoors: he knew the coast highway from a rider's perspective—sometimes using actual examples for his class to imagine: *We're going to do an uphill climb. Increase the tension on the bike when I tell you. Pretend this is Cascade Head. Know how good you'll feel when you reach the top.*

She also knew that he preferred jazz to rock and roll, but that the darling had requested peppier music to ride to. Patricia actually missed the Al Jarreau mixed with Branford Marsalis. It had provided a great middle period to the class.

When the spinning hour was up, and all the regulars had come in, the heavyset cop told the aerobics instructor to put a closed sign on the door, and lock it. Then they took people one by one into the manager's office, and asked questions.

The heavyset cop remained out front mostly, to deter conversation, Patricia supposed. He watched them all too closely too, and the mirrors didn't help. They allowed him to see everything in that large exercise area, the slightest gesture, the smallest twitch.

After people spoke to the blue-eyed cop in the office, they were allowed to leave. Exercisers were interviewed in the order that they arrived. Obviously someone had kept very careful track.

What it meant was that by the time Patricia was called, the gym rats were gone, but most of the class remained. The aerobics instructor had called her boss, and he had come down to lock up. Patricia also got a sense that he wanted to speak to the police himself.

When the heavyset cop said her name, Patricia got up, legs wobbly. She almost forgot her purse and gym bag, and grabbed them as an afterthought. Then she walked past the mirrors to the office where she had only been one time: the day she had signed up. That day she had been carrying an extra 80 pounds and even though she had dressed to hide it, it had been painfully obvious in the small room.

This time, the room's contours seemed more suited to her frame. The blue-eyed cop closed the door, asked her if she minded that the conversation was recorded, and then asked her to sit.

"This is just routine," he said.

It didn't seem routine, but she didn't say that. She had promised herself out front that she would volunteer nothing, and if he spent more than five minutes asking questions—the average time he had spent with the others—she would call an attorney just on principle.

"How well did you know Tom Ansara, Ms. Taylor?" The cop sat behind the messy manager's desk and folded his hands on top of a pile of papers that clearly didn't belong to him. His blue eyes seemed even more intense in the small space.

"He was my spinning instructor."

"For how long?"

"Eighteen months."

"You know that number precisely?"

She nodded. "I started my exercise program with his class."

"Was it effective?"

"The program?"

"The class."

She shrugged. "It motivated me."

"I understand you lost a lot of weight due to Mr. Ansara."

She almost choked. She felt a flush climb up her neck, her face, and she couldn't stop it. It was as if this man, this cop, had seen into her mind, had read each secret thought, knew how Tom had inspired her.

Knew about the revenge.

"I don't know if you can blame Tom," she said at last.

Blue-eyes raised his eyebrows ever so slightly. The expression gave his face a warmth it hadn't had before. "Blame? I would think you'd be proud of the loss."

"I am," she said, and almost repeated *I* am. But she didn't. She wasn't going to give anything.

"And Tom helped you."

"The spinning class helped me." The flush had receded from her cheeks. Now her skin was cold. She wondered if she had turned pale, and how he would read this.

"You haven't asked what happened to Tom."

"I figured you would tell me."

He studied her for a moment. "He's still in the work-out room. Would you like to take a look?"

"God no!" The response came out of her mouth before she could stop it. What was this man thinking, offering her the chance to look at a dead body? Not just any dead body, but the dead body of a man she had known, and fantasized about, however inappropriately.

"How tall are you, Ms. Taylor?"

The question so startled her that she had to think before responding. "Five-four." How did that relate to Tom's death? How did any of it?

She had forgotten to look at the clock and now she was afraid to, afraid it would seem insensitive, afraid it would make her even more suspicious than she probably already was.

"All right," he said. "We're done."

She remained sitting for a moment, disoriented, as he probably wanted her to be. She opened her mouth once, then closed it.

"Although," he said, "you should probably tell me how to get ahold of you. I'm sure it's here in the gym's records, but it's easier if you tell me."

She did. She told him her work phone and her home phone, and even what hours she would be in both places. He gave her a business card with his name on it. She didn't know policemen had business cards, but apparently they did. This one had the city's symbol on it, and then Detective David

Huckleby. It was such a jokey name, a rural cop name, that in any other context, she would have smiled.

Instead she pocketed the card and stood. He stood too, came up beside her, so that he could open the door.

As he reached for the knob, she said, “You still didn’t tell me how Tom died.”

“I didn’t?” He let go of the knob. “Careless of me.” When it hadn’t been at all. He had wanted her to ask. He had confused her, disoriented her, and then wondered if she would remember to ask. She knew that much. It was some kind of game. Maybe she should have called a lawyer after all.

“Tom’s neck was broken, Ms. Taylor,” Detective Huckleby said. “We think someone wrapped an arm around his neck and snapped it.”

He paused, watching her face. She felt her heart beating hard. She couldn’t picture it. She couldn’t picture someone grabbing Tom like that.

“You know the grip,” Huckleby said. “It’s the one they teach in the self defense classes here.”

She had taken one of those classes just the month before. The instructor had been from out of town, a burly man who taught self-defense all over the country. He had used her as his model victim. She had stood in front of the class, felt his fingers on her neck as he positioned her, then remained very still while his arm encircled her throat. With a sharp movement of the forearm, and a backward pull on the hair, he had said, a neck could be broken, snapped, in a heartbeat.

She hadn't known why anyone would want this information. But the class had been in self-defense. And sometimes, she knew from her television-watching experience, self-defense meant only one person got out alive.

Huckleby was watching her, waiting for her reaction. He had known she had been in the class. He had obviously seen the sign-up list.

He touched her arm, felt her biceps, the muscle clearly developed beneath a thin layer of skin. His touch was gentle and, if she hadn't been in such a state of heightened awareness, she would have thought it accidental.

"Will you miss him?" Huckleby asked.

Her mouth was dry. The feeling of guilt had grown stronger. "I'll miss his class," she said. It was the only thing she could tell him. It was the only truth she knew.

"What a sad epitaph for a man you've known for eighteen months, a man who was proud of helping you lose weight."

"I didn't know him," she said, hearing as she spoke how defensive the words sounded. "I just took a class from him."

"I hear he had a thing for pretty women."

She laughed without mirth. It was an involuntary reaction, one that had been trained in over all the years, all the weight. "That wouldn't have included me."

"It does now," Huckleby said softly.

She felt the smile, the inappropriate smile, leave her face. "I was obese when I came into his class," she said. "I couldn't even pedal the damn bike with the resistance turned off for more than thirty seconds at a stretch. Then I'd pant for five minutes and try again."

"Tenacity can be attractive."

"Maybe," she said. "But you don't forget how someone looked when you met them."

You don't forget that not-quite-sympathetic look in the eye, the disgust when he thought no one was looking. You don't forget any of that.

She thought those last two sentences, but had enough self control to prevent them from coming out of her mouth.

"I don't think you know how far you've come, Ms. Taylor," Huckleby said softly.

"Oh, I do," she said. "And Tom knew it too." She glanced at the door. "Can I go now?"

His smile was gentle. If she had met him in other circumstances, she might even have thought it kind. "Sure."

She let herself out and glanced at the clock. She had been in there twenty minutes. So much for proper resolutions.

"Ms. Taylor?"

She turned. He was holding her purse and gym bag. She swallowed. "Thanks," she said, taking them from him. She bent her head and walked to the door. The gym's owner, a muscular man who looked as if he spent too much time on the bench press, let her out. She took the stairs, slowly, thinking as she did so, that she would never hear Tom again, never hear that odd hitch in his voice, the way it caught when he got into the rhythm of the workout, the way it soared above the music.

His body was on the floor of the exercise room, his neck tilted at an odd angle. She wondered what he looked like, if he still seemed like a Greek god, even in his death repose. And then she shuddered. She would never be able to go in that room again.

She put her bag and purse in the car, and locked it. Then she took off at a run down the parking lot, not because she was frightened, but because she needed to burn off the fear she had felt.

She needed the exercise, and she had to prove to herself that she could do it without Tom.

***

SHE WOKE in the middle of the night with an ache in her heart and tears in her eyes. She wanted a piece of chocolate cake so badly that it hurt. Fortunately, she lived in a small town that didn't have an all night grocery store, and she didn't keep cake mixes in her small apartment.

Comfort food. She wanted comfort food because she needed comforting.

She heard her own voice, speaking to Huckleby: *I didn't know him. I just took a class from him.*

But if it were that simple, why couldn't she sleep? Her mother hadn't been able to sleep in the first few months after her father died. Neither had she, if the truth be told. The brain was busy trying to process the loss. Too busy to sleep more than a few hours at a time.

That had been when she had put on the serious weight. Chocolate cake in the middle of the night, topped with vanilla ice cream. Or Cool Whip. Or Hershey's syrup.

Her mouth watered. She needed something comforting. Now. Never deny the cravings, she knew that much. But she couldn't afford to fall back into bad habits just because her spinning class instructor was dead.

She wondered why the local best-selling psychiatrist would say about this. Probably recommend therapy. Probably report her to the police. She could hear it now: *She had a revenge fantasy about the man. Perhaps she acted it out. Perhaps she stalked him.*

She sat down at the kitchen table she had bought at a Discount Furniture Store and assembled herself, then put her hands in her short-cropped hair. If she were honest with herself, she knew that she could have killed him. If her revenge fantasy had taken a different, more harmful twist. If she had gotten to the acting-out stage—which she had. She had been planning to come in that night, to continue the seduction. She had heard how willing he was to date women at the club. She had known about his preference for the sleek muscular women, the clear athletes. She had planned to use that to her benefit.

And the cop had seen it. He had seen it, and something about her height made him dismiss her.

But he shouldn't have. Patricia hadn't seen the body, but she knew the room, and she knew one thing: Tom liked to sit on the floor and talk to people. She could imagine how someone like her could have killed him:

He would have been sitting cross-legged on the polished wood floor in the center of the room, holding forth on the value of good nutrition or how so many reps burn so much fat, when someone came up behind him, put him in the stranglehold and pulled until he couldn't breathe. Then he fell back, sprawling across the floor, his neck bent at the odd angle. Simple. Easy. So simple and easy even a short person could have done it.

She wished she could mention that to Huckleby without raising suspicion, but she couldn't. All she could do was listen for the gossip, read the local papers, and pretend that Tom's death had no effect on her life.

***

LIKE A WOMAN who had just fallen off a horse, she made herself go to the gym the following night. Getting back in the saddle, she had whispered to herself, and while that wasn't entirely accurate, it was good enough.

The owner sat behind the desk, paperwork spread in front of him. A big sign, written in black Magic Marker, announced that all classes had been canceled until further notice. He saw her stare at it, and said, "We can't have the room until the investigation's done."

She wasn't sure if that was supposed to make her feel better or worse, so she just nodded, and went into the locker room to change. Another woman was standing near the row of sinks, reading a sign newly taped to the wall. The sign was computer generated and it mentioned a trust fund, set up by the gym, for Tom Ansara's daughter.

Patricia felt a jolt. "I didn't know he had a daughter."

The woman nodded. Patricia had seen her around, but had never bothered to learn her name. "Sixteen. She's being raised by the mother in Seattle. But he was here, trying to earn money for her college. Now she may never go."

Patricia almost asked what happened to scholarships, but thought that too crass. Instead she made a sympathetic noise and changed into her sweats. She went into the gym proper, and used the newest StairMaster set on high for an hour, until sweat poured off her. While she worked out, she noticed that only the regulars were here. The dilettantes, the ones who showed up every January or once a month or after a particularly big meal, hadn't come at all. And that was unusual. Every night usually had one.

As she marched up and down a make-believe flight of stairs, she was conscious of the room behind her, hidden by a row of racquetball courts and bleachers, now cordoned off by the local police. The more she marched and sweated, the more she focused on that room. She wanted to see it, wanted to know, perhaps, if he were really dead.

The room had mirrors covering three walls and a row of windows covering the fourth. The windows overlooked the free weight area. When she got off the StairMaster, and grabbed her sweat towel, wrapping it around her neck, she meandered into the free weight area as if her movement were part of her routine.

The windows showed a darkened room, lit only by the lights reflected in the mirrors. There was no chalk outline of a body on the floor—she had read somewhere that Hollywood made that up and the police never used it. She just hadn't believed it to be true—and the special spinning bikes were lined up against the back wall, just like usual, waiting for class members to wheel them toward the middle. Beside them were the pile of step mats, and next to that the boxy audio system that had threatened to ruin her hearing.

Nothing was different except the yellow police tape covering the door, and the sign attached: *Closed by Order of the Seavy Village Police.* She shuddered, wishing, somehow that she had never heard about his death. That she had stayed away as her weight came down and her revenge fantasy demanded its own conclusion, and when she came back and forgot to ask about Tom, people forgot to tell her about him, so that she would assume he had moved away, or lost his job, or found employment that required use of his mind. But she couldn't pretend those things in retrospect, and she couldn't drop the disappointment she felt that somehow, she had been cheated of something.

"Any clues?" A male voice behind her made her jump.

She turned. Detective Huckleby was standing so close to her that he almost pressed her against the window.

"No," she said.

"Strange," he said. "A room is always a room, even after something awful happened in it. Unless you know, the room is no different."

She had had that thought before. Apartments and hotel rooms always made her wonder when she first arrived if anyone had died in them. She had always thought she would be able to tell by some subtle vibration, something that had altered because of the death.

But she felt no such vibration from the gym, none from the exercise room at all, and she was surprised.

"I didn't think any of the class members would show up tonight," he said.

"I didn't just go to class," she said. "This is my routine."

"Routine." He spoke softly, as if he were musing.

Her heart had started to pound again. "I lost my weight, detective, through exercise. I have to continue that, particularly now—"

"Now that your instructor is dead?"

She nodded.

"So he did have an influence on your weight loss."

She licked her lips. "He inspired me." That much was true.

"Who's going to inspire you now?"

She met his gaze. Electric blue. Neon blue. Like she imagined Paul Newman's eyes would be in person. "I guess I have to," she said.

"Always tough," he said. "It's always better if the motivation comes from the outside."

She wasn't sure if he was speaking of exercise now, or if he was speaking of murder. Would he be happier if the killer came from outside Seavy Village? Or outside the gym? She swallowed. She had been so focused on herself, on Tom's death, that she hadn't thought about the reality of murder. The fact that a murder victim had to have a murderer.

"Are you done with your exercise?" he asked.

"Do you want to interrogate me again?"

To her surprise, he laughed. "If you thought that was an interrogation," he said, "I don't want to put you through a real one."

She saw no humor in it. Yesterday had been a bad day, a day she did not want to repeat.

He must have seen that on her face, for his smile faded. "Sorry," he said. "You're not a suspect."

"At this time," she said.

He half shrugged. "I suppose." He looked around at the empty bleachers, the slouching owner pouring over the papers behind the reception desk. "I was hoping to buy you coffee and ask a few questions about the gym."

"Me?"

He faced her, his eyes meeting hers. "Well," he said. "Actually anyone from the class who bothered to show up tonight. You're the only one."

"I thought you didn't expect any of us to show up tonight."

"I figured it would only be the exercise addicts."

It was her turn to smile, hers rueful. "It is."

He nodded once. "Coffee?"

"Water or Gatorade. Coffee's a diuretic."

"Hmm," he said. "And that's bad?"

She looked at him, uncertain if that were a real joke. She supposed it was. It seemed strange to joke in front of a room where a man had been murdered.

"There's a deli and juice bar upstairs," she said, not sure why she agreed.

"Lead the way," he said.

"Let me change," she said. 'I'll meet you there."

"I suppose you want carrot juice."

"Actually," she said. "I want bottled water. And maybe an apple."

"Done."

She pushed past him and went to the lady's locker room. Her hands were shaking and she was wondering what she was doing. He was a cop investigating a murder, and he wanted to talk to her a second time, informally. She felt as if she were doing something wrong, as if she should get on the phone and ask for a lawyer or not show up or go upstairs and ask what he was charging her with. But all of that seemed melodramatic and unnecessary and a bit rude.

After a quick—very quick—shower, she put on her street clothes—a cheap cotton sweater and a pair of faded jeans. She left on her tennies, and kept her gym bag in the locker. She saw no reason to spend too much time with him.

The restaurant upstairs had gone through many formats in the eighteen months she had worked out in the gym. The first and most appalling had been the steak joint that served its meat thick and charbroiled. The next had been a vegetarian restaurant with poorly made, tasteless 1970 cuisine. Then different taverns came in after that, and now, finally, the deli, with its smoothie and juice bars. This new place was the only one that got the regulars from the gym. Sometimes they ran up the stairs, got a small sandwich and a fruit drink and then went back down to work out some more.

She had come up more than once with a novel, usually science fiction, and had eaten, alone, most often the taco deli sandwich made with fat-free refried beans. It had flavor, and it was filling and it didn't have a lot of calories, all of which counted in its favor. The seats were comfortable, and the staff congenial, never asking her to move when she finished her meal.

Now she went up to find herself and Huckleby the only clients. The lights were out in the far section of the deli, and a single employee, an older woman whom Patricia had never seen before, cleaned behind the counter.

A bottled water and the fruit plate waited for her. Huckleby had a cup of coffee and a shortbread cookie.

"That's a lot of food."

"You looked like you could use it."

How many years had she waited for someone to say that only to find it was someone she didn't want to impress. She slipped into the chair, and opened the bottle of water.

"You had questions."

He nodded. "Tell me what you can about Tom."

"We had this conversation yesterday."

"Yesterday I knew less than I do today."

"Oh?" She took a long sip. She had been thirsty, which meant she had let herself get dehydrated. Careless of her.

"Yeah," he said.

"Like what?"

He broke the shortbread cookie in half, then broke a half into smaller pieces. "No," he said. "I get to ask the questions first."

"I already told you about Tom."

"You told me what you know. And that was official. Now I want to know what you suspect."

Suspect. Strange word. Was she supposed to tell this man that she thought Tom Ansara was self-involved and rather stupid, that he had an eye for pretty women, and no real empathy for anyone who wouldn't look like a perfect match for him? Or should she tell him about her suspicions of Tom's performance in bed?

"I think he biked a lot," she said.

Huckleby raised an amused eyebrow. "Gee. We missed that."

She felt color rise in her cheeks. "No," she said. "I mean biked all over the city, maybe over the area."

"That's not gossip."

"You want gossip?"

"Yes."

"Talk to the aerobics instructor then. She collects it."

He leaned back and studied her. "That was harsh. You don't like her?"

"I don't know her."

"It amazes me that you could come to a gym for eighteen months and not know anyone."

"I came to work out."

"People usually make friends in places like this."

"Not with fat people."

"Why? They make friends with fat people everywhere else."

She picked up her fork and stabbed an orange slice with it, feeling a momentary victory when some of the juice shot across the table toward him. "I understand it," she said. "At least I do now. Most people who are more than 20 pounds overweight don't stay. It had nothing to do with discipline and everything to do with effort. It takes a lot of work to move a normal weight, but add extra weight on top of it, and a fat person is working twice, sometimes three times harder than everyone else. Most people don't have the discipline, and they leave."

"So you don't make friends with fat people at the gym either?"

"I thought we already established that I don't make friends," she said.

His gaze seemed a little too sharp for a moment, as if her admission was an admission to something else as well. "I'm sure you do in your personal life."

She had a few friends, people she talked to, but no one she confided in. She hadn't confided in anyone for a very long time. Not even her brother. They talked about casual things. She supposed that counted as friendship.

And she had a lot of acquaintances on-line. She kept a board running behind her work at all time, and answered her e-mail when it showed up. She closed out her nightly sessions in a chat room, each night devoted to a different subject, just to keep her mind active.

The silence between them had grown. Finally, she said, "I thought you wanted to hear about Tom."

"And I thought you didn't gossip."

She ate the orange slice. It was sour. She took a sip of water to cover the taste. "I discovered in the last twenty-four hours how little I knew about him. Like the daughter."

"There is no daughter," Huckleby said.

She set the bottle of water down very deliberately. "But the sign—"

"He told people there was a daughter, and the very kind folks in Seavy Village have started a fund. But I investigated, and I can tell you, there is no daughter. No ex-wife. No acrimonious divorce. There isn't even a Tom Ansara until he came to Seavy Village."

So there was more to this than just the gym. That relieved her somehow, made the thought of murder caused by people who frequented her safe place go away.

"All of his relationships lasted a few weeks at most," Huckleby said, "so consider yourself lucky he didn't make a pass at you."

Such a quaint old-fashioned phrase "make a pass" was. She almost smiled. But a part of her brain, the suspicious part, remained distant.

"Why are you telling me all this?"

"Because," he said. "I figured if I opened up, you would. And you look like a lady who has something to get off her chest."

She felt her eyes widen, and wished she could stop them, wished she had more control than she did. Now, when she lied, he would know it. "I've told you everything I can," she said.

He stared at her for a moment. "Pity."

"I don't hold any keys," she said. "I'd tell you if I did."

"Would you?" he asked, then dropped a ten on the table and stood. By the time she got to her feet, he was gone.

***

ALL THAT NIGHT and as she ate her solitary bowl of cereal the next morning, she kept telling herself that it was silly to feel like she was failing Huckleby somehow. She didn't even know him, didn't know anything about him. All she knew was that he wanted information on Tom's death, and she had none.

In fact, she had even less than she had had before. She had believed the stories about Tom around the gym, had thought him a divorced man with a conventional past. Now, perhaps, he didn't have one, and he, not the murderer, had violated the safety of the gym, of Seavy Village itself.

Blaming the victim, they called it. But she knew that things were never as clear-cut as they seemed. Apparently, so did Huckleby.

When she got to work, her schedule was light: some routine maintenance of a few sites, and monitoring of a few others. She opened the usual chat room where she hung out when things were slow, but couldn't concentrate.

Her brother was in his office, talking loudly on the phone. He wanted to expand their service beyond the coast, to move into the valley. It would entail hiring additional staff, getting more lines, working more computers. It would be a nightmare for her, but so far she hadn't tried to talk him out of it.

Rather than listen to him argue with another of his friends over his plans, she opened her window. The morning breeze smelled of sea salt and fish. It was cold, but she didn't mind. She needed something else to concentrate on.

But her attention kept wandering back to Huckleby's words about Tom, about his secrets, and she finally succumbed. She knew where he lived: she had followed him there, once, early on, so that she could have a setting to imagine her revenge. Actually sitting in her car on that cold November night, watching him shaded against his window as he moved through his apartment, made her feel like a voyeur, a stalker, something she didn't want to be. So, even though she felt an urge to follow him at other times, she never had.

Still, she used his name and address to access his driver's license. Some schlub had gotten in trouble, in Oregon, for placing all the DMV records on the Internet and, even though he had removed them, Patricia had captured the file, thinking some day it would be useful.

It was. With Tom's driver's license number, she was able to get into his credit report, and that, in turn, gave her his social security number. It didn't belong to Tom Ansara, but to someone else, an elderly woman in Pittsburgh. Apparently he had stolen the number. But he had used it for a very long time and through it, and his credit report, she saw a life of transience, a man of many names and, as she dug, several petty crimes, mostly involving drugs, theft, and a certain roughness with women.

That last made a shudder run through her. Her revenge fantasy had been too subtle for this man. It might have turned on her. No matter how strong she was, she might not have been able to overcome his athlete's quickness. She knew that much.

Her fantasy could have ended badly. For her.

At that, she rested her head on her arms and made herself breathe. How foolish she had become. How obsessed with a man she hadn't even known. She had even mourned him, in her own way, this man she had made up.

The door to her office opened, and her brother came in. She recognized him by his footsteps.

"You okay?"

She raised her head. Her brother still carried all the weight he had put on as he aged. Sometimes he eyed her new form as if it were a reproach to him. But she liked him at this weight. It gave him a cuddly warmth that he hadn't had when he was thinner.

"Yeah," she said. "Just tired."

He nodded. All he knew about Tom was what the rest of the town knew: that he had been murdered in thc gym. The next day, her brother had asked her if it was safe for her to return. When she assured him it was, he had said, "I hope so," and she knew, with that terse phrase, that the conversation was closed.

He pulled up the only other chair, a folding chair she kept unfolded in the corner. It squeaked as he sat on it. "Look," he said. "If I manage to get more business, we might have to leave Seavy Village. This just isn't a good place to do business, not if we start focusing on the valley."

Her heart was pounding. She didn't want to leave. She loved it here. "I won't go," she said.

"I know. I was thinking, maybe you could be in charge of our coastal lines."

That meant customer relations. It meant working alone. "Let's wait," she said. "Talk about this when the changes become real."

"It's getting closer every day, Patty," he said. Her brother was the only person who could call her Patty and get away with it.

"I know," she said. "I just don't want to think about it now."

***

AND SHE DIDN'T, not until she was on the silly StairMaster for the second night in a row. Sweat was dripping between her breasts, and the back of her neck was damp. The club's televisions were all tuned to a football game, and their sound was on, as well as the latest Rod Stewart CD at full blast. She was surprised she could hear herself think. But the noise blurred, and she found her mind wandering, going over her brother's words, trying to see if there was any reality in the changes he was discussing for his business.

Then it hit her, what he had said. *Seavy Village isn't a good place to do business*. And it wasn't. The town was small, many of its residents unskilled workers with low-paying jobs or retirees who lived on a fixed income. The tourists were seasonal: summers, mostly, with a few spikes around the holidays. Yet Tom had been here for eighteen months, maybe more. He hadn't had a single arrest, which, considering his record before he arrived, was spectacular, and she remembered nothing that made him seem as if he had been on drugs. What had he found that kept him here? It certainly hadn't been the spinning class. And whatever it had been, someone had considered it worth killing for.

Pretend this is Cascade Head, he would say. *Know how good you'll feel when you reach the top.*

And all the other sites on the coast route. He would mention them, use them in his class. But he always came back to Cascade Head, as if it were important, to them, and to him.

For one long stretch of her workout, she considered buying a bike and exploring the places he had mentioned, searching. But for what, she didn't know. And she had never searched for anything. She had no idea how to go about it.

She had to talk to Huckleby. She wondered if he would think she was crazy, all the work she had done on this. He was going to want to know why and the answer she had was really no answer at all, just a truth she was beginning to discover:

That obsession, once begun, did not end easily. That losing it felt a lot like losing love.

***

THE POLICE STATION, tucked in a back road behind the post office, was a 1960s building, all metal and sand-colored brick. Its gray tile floors were spotless, and the walls had recently been painted white. She felt oddly betrayed by its cleanliness. Somehow she had expected the grit she had seen portrayed on TV.

When she asked for Huckleby, the woman at the desk—statuesque, her uniform accenting rather than hiding her figure—nodded toward the only man sitting in a sea of desks. Patricia wasn't sure how she missed him, except that she hadn't expect this place to be this way, and somehow hadn't expected him to look so lost and all alone, bathed in the fog-gray light filtering in from the cross-hatched windows.

The smell, she noted as she walked toward him, was strong: burned coffee and stale sweat, the kind of smell that a person never got used to. It wasn't until she was standing over him that he looked up, and from the movement of his lips, she guessed he had been planning to make a comment to someone else when he edited himself for her.

"I didn't expect to see you again," he said, and kicked a green and metal desk chair in her direction. She sat gingerly on it, half expecting it to squeal as her folding chair did when her brother sat on it.

His comment was strange given the size of the town they lived in. They would see each other from time to time, probably had already and just hadn't known it, until now.

She licked her lips. "I did some digging."

"Oh?" He was giving her his full attention. The file before him was closed and pushed aside, his hands threaded on the desk like a man who was patiently waiting to hear something he didn't already know.

"The name Ansara is unusual," she said, knowing that this was an inane way to start. "There was a movie star in the late sixties and early seventies named Michael Ansara. He looked something like Tom."

"Yeah," Huckleby said, his tone dry. "I can't decide if Tom's favorite movie was *Sometimes a Great Notion* or that awful television remake of *Dracula.*"

In spite of herself, she smiled. She ducked her head so that he wouldn't see how amused she was. This was serious, after all.

"But I did even more digging. I found out about his record."

His eyebrows went up. "You're good," he said. "Care to share with me how you did that?"

She had thought this through before she had come, and now she told him the story she had planned: it was the entire truth minus the driver's license records. Even though anyone could get DMV records simply by writing to the division, she felt almost criminal using them, even more criminal for storing them. Still, if he asked, she would tell him. She only hoped he wouldn't ask.

He didn't, but he was leaning forward now, looking at her with a mixture of puzzlement and respect.

"I would have left it at that," she said, "except I got to wondering, what would a man like that be doing in Seavy Village for so long?"

"Staying clean?" Huckleby said. Clearly he'd thought of that too.

"Maybe," she said. "But when he did spinning class, he outlined bike routes, something we could imagine while our feet were hopelessly circling." She took a piece of paper out of her battered purse. "Here are the places he mentioned, and the way he mentioned them. Cascade Head was the one he focused on, but I always thought that was because it was so high. But he could have used the Van Duzer Corridor for the same thing, or maybe something in the Cascades, and he didn't. He just kept coming back to this one, over and over, like his mind was stuck."

Huckleby glanced at the paper. "You're quite specific. How do you remember what he said?"

She flushed. "I was in his class for a long time. It got boring after a while. You did anything you could to concentrate. I focused on his words. He repeated himself a lot."

He tapped the paper against his hand. "Nice work," he said, tapping the paper against his hand. "I knew you'd remember something if you tried hard enough."

"Is it important?" she asked.

"Important?" He kept a grip on the paper while he reached for the phone. "It's the missing piece."

***

SHE DIDN'T HEAR anything for three days. Every time she thought of calling the station, she made herself do something else. The danger with obsession, the website told her, was that once one went away, another sometimes arose in its place. Too many, and a person needed therapy. A single one, and perhaps the person needed more to do with her life.

More than computers, exercise and solitary meals. More than ducking her head to avoid conversations every time she went to the gym.

She joined the aerobics class and made a point, that night, of learning everyone's names. She told her brother that she thought his expansion a bad idea at this stage in their business, and he was so pleased that she used the word "their" that he didn't even try to argue with her. He asked her what she thought the business needed, and she told him all the things she had never said. To her surprise, he made a list and walked out of her office, studying it, ready, he said, to make changes.

On the third day, the local 5:15 newscast announced that a suspect was being held in the murder of Tom Ansara. A man, with a name Patricia didn't recognize, an out-of-towner, as the announcer called him with obvious relief, who had business with Ansara that predated his arrival in Seavy Village.

She was surprised she hadn't heard from Huckleby. She would have thought that, as a courtesy, he would have told her first.

And then she wondered where that assumption came from. She had provided a small bit of information in an on-going investigation.

He owed her nothing. She owed him nothing. And that's where things would always stand.

***

THE DETAILS came out bit by bit, not in the local paper which saw itself as a promoter of tourism on the coast and as such tried to cover up the seamier stuff, but in the *Oregonian* which followed the entire case with an interest unusual in their non-Portland coverage.

Tom Ansara's real name was Andrew Thomas. He had arrests in several states for drug crimes, most of which were minor possession violations. But only two states had more serious charges against him. One, in an unlikely connection with a group of art thieves operating in Los Angeles. Ansara fled the area after some Mirós, Picassos, a Jackson Pollack and an original Dali were stolen from a home in Brentwood. He came to Oregon, took a new name, and hid, careful to stay away from Seavy Village's minor drug trade, and managing, somehow, to break off his relations with women before things became too serious.

He hadn't had anything to do with the art heists, had merely stumbled on them in the course of his other shady dealings, and knew, somehow, who was involved. Police assumed he dated one of the thieves, hearing the plans for the Brentwood theft from her. But the heat on that was high, and someone threatened him. When he came to Oregon, he made notes of all he knew, and buried them on Cascade Head.

He had mailed a letter to himself the day he died—obviously he had been worried, perhaps he had seen his killer, a man named Will Garetson. In the letter, Tom explained that he had hidden a box, and how far it was from Highway 101, and he gave a detailed description of the unusual tree and rock formation near the burial site. Unfortunately, he had left out what part of 101 he was talking about. When Patricia—"a private citizen" as the papers called her—had come forward, she had provided the missing piece of information: where exactly the box was. The police looked on Cascade Head at the correct distance from 101, found the distinctive tree and rock formation, and proceeded to dig.

They found the box, and in it, the names of the people involved in the heist, a tape recording with their voices on it planning that heist, and a list of the items that they had hoped to take. Also in the box was a note about the reasons Tom had hidden in Oregon: It wasn't because his conscience had finally gotten to him about the heist or because he had been discovered by the thieves. It was because, on the two jobs the thieves performed before his disappearance, they had killed security guards, and Tom was beginning to fear that killing for sport was becoming the reason behind the heists, not the theft itself.

So he vanished, and it took them a long time to trace him. He made two mistakes: he took a regular job, and he kept the old social security number. Eventually Garetson found him. In fact, the article said, the man who killed Tom had been the self-defense instructor at the gym a few weeks before Tom's death. Because instructors were rarely in the building at the same time, Tom hadn't seen him. Garetson had discovered Tom's routine, where he lived, and who he had offended in Seavy Village and had apparently decided the best way to kill the man was do it at the gym, where all the women he slept with would then become suspects.

It would have worked if it weren't for that letter, and Detective Huckleby, who felt there was something wrong with this case from the beginning.

Patricia read the articles with avid interest, worried when she learned how easy it had been for a killer to infiltrate her small town and target a man, calmer when she realized one of the reasons the man had been targeted was because of his own behavior.

It took a week for the *Oregonian* to print all the articles, but when it was done, and Garetson was in jail awaiting trial, she felt as if it were over. Or at least part of it. She could still remember the touch of his hands on her neck as he held her in place, using her to demonstrate to the rest of the self-defense class how to do the chokehold. When his arm wrapped around her throat, she had thought how easy it would be for him to squeeze, how easy it would be for her to die.

Apparently, he had killed Tom with no struggle. Apparently, she had been right. It had been easy, after all.

***

So she went back to her life, changed as it was. Her brother gave her more responsibility at the IP and she found a jogging partner, a woman whom she had spoken to a few times at the gym and felt an affinity for. They were developing a friendship composed of short conversations followed by a mile or more of gasping silence. She found that she liked talking with someone. She actually looked forward to it.

By the end of the second week, she made it through two days without thinking of Tom. Then Huckleby walked into her office. He leaned against the door, smiled at her, and let his blue eyes draw her in.

"Do you do lunch?" he asked.

"Only on every other Thursday," she said, and was surprised at the tartness of her own reply.

His smile widened into a grin. "I'm buying."

She went with him to the health food restaurant next door. He ordered the only meal with beef in it—a shredded beef taco concoction made with cream cheese instead of sour cream—and she had their homemade tomato soup and fresh sour dough bread.

"You never followed up on the case," he said after the food was served.

"You didn't keep me informed."

He took a bite from the taco, and half the cream cheese fell out. He set the food down. "I was a little busy."

"But you got him," she said.

"We got him. It's up to the L.A. cops to get the rest." He sounded relieved at that.

"More excitement than Seavy village is used to," She said.

"More than we want," he replied. Then he put an elbow on the table, and watched her. She had never had anyone watch her eat before.

"You know," he said. "In all the times we talked, you never did tell me how you felt about him."

"About Tom?" she asked, stalling. She put her soup spoon down, and picked up the bread, shredding it.

"Yes."

She shrugged. "He was my spinning instructor."

"And?"

There was no harm in telling him now. No harm in saying anything. She felt herself flush. She had to look away. "And I hated him."

He let out a slow whistle, as if he hadn't expected it. "Because he was a drill sergeant?"

She shook her head. The soup was nearly gone. She had made a mess of the bread. There were crumbs on her side of the napkin. She stared at them instead of looking Huckleby in the eye.

"Because of how he looked at me, in the beginning. Like I offended him just by being in his presence."

To her surprise, Huckleby took her hand. She raised her head, saw him looking at her with empathy, not disgust. She wanted to look away, but couldn't.

"Do you know how many times you told me that fat people get treated differently?"

"They do," she said.

"You're no longer fat," he said.

"I always will be." With her free hand she tapped her chest. "Inside. I'll always remember how it feels. Like an alcoholic. I'll always be a fat person crammed into a skinny shell."

"If you want to be," he said. "No one sees you that way any more. No one treats you that way. The loathing I hear when I'm around you comes from you."

He said the words softly, gently, to lessen their sting. But they still hurt. She blinked, startled. No one had ever talked that way to her before. But then, she hadn't let anyone talk to her, really talk to her, for years.

"I don't want to treat anyone else that way," she said.

"But you do," he said. "You assume all the rest of us will look at you with that same disgust that Ansara had, and you hate us in advance."

"I don't hate you," she said.

He smiled and squeezed her hand. "It's a start at least."

"Of what?" she asked.

He shrugged. "I don't know. Friendship, maybe something more. If you're willing."

She had never fantasized about him, not in this way, never imagined what he would sound like in bed, never allowed herself to think a man like this one would even be interested. He was a person to her, not a Greek god who looked down on the less-than-perfect with complete disdain, like Tom had been. Only Tom hadn't been. He had been as imperfect as she was. It just hadn't been apparent from the way he looked, the way he dressed, the way he spoke. Only his eyes had showed it, and only if someone paid attention.

She felt a little floaty hit of adrenaline, like she used get in her early spinning classes after she had been on the bike a while. Just when she thought she would be ready to quit, something in her body would adjust and she would feel slightly dizzy, slightly high. A little afraid and a bit proud of herself at the same time.

Friendship. Something more. If she was willing.

"All right," she said, and squeezed Huckleby's hand.

There was no longer a need for fantasy. The need for fantasy had made her blind to the realities around her. Some of those realities could have harmed her—the arm around her neck, the same arm that had crushed Tom's throat—and others could have helped her, allowed her to see that things were different now, that she was different and perhaps, she always would be.

She was no longer spinning her wheels on a stationary bike. She had been moving forward for a long time; and she had finally noticed.

About the Author

INTERNATIONAL BESTSELLING writer Kristine Kathryn Rusch has published fiction in every genre. She has been nominated for three Edgar Awards, two Shamus Awards, and an Anthony Award. She has won the *Ellery Queen* Reader's Choice Award twice. She has also published award-winning mystery novels under the name Kris Nelscott. For more about her work, go to kristinekathrynrusch.com.

Also by
Kristine Kathryn Rusch

Bleed Through
Snipers
Five Mystery Stories (a collection)
Five Diverse Detectives (a collection)

The Retrieval Artist Series:

The Disappeared
Extremes
Consequences
Buried Deep
Paloma
Recovery Man
Duplicate Effort
Anniversary Day
Blowback

The Smokey Dalton Series (as Kris Nelscott):

A Dangerous Road
Smoke-Filled Rooms
Thin Walls
Stone Cribs
War at Home
Days of Rage

www.ingramcontent.com/pod-product-compliance
Lightning Source LLC
LaVergne TN
LVHW090939080826
845145LV00003B/814

* 9 7 8 0 6 1 5 7 7 1 3 5 9 *